I0593733

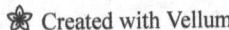 Created with Vellum

DROP DEAD IN RED

LIVIA DAY

DROP DEAD IN RED

SYLVIA DAY

1

THE TRICK TO LIVING IN TASMANIA IS YOU'RE NEVER THAT far from a mountain.

If we stopped what we were doing and went 'ahhh' every time we saw a glorious bit of scenery, we'd never get anything done.

I've had a tough couple of years, and I like to think that it's hardened me a little. I'm no longer the old Samantha, the squishy soft-centre Sam who thought the best of everyone. And yet...

Well, I defy you to drive past the lookout point to the Sleeping Beauty mountain range and feel nothing. If anything is 'ahhh'-worthy, that is.

Today, I didn't have time for scenery. It was a quick drop off, then back to work in my boss's borrowed car. Still got to enjoy the glorious view of grey-blue mountains, curved into almost the right kind of shape to be a sleeping person.

When I was a kid, I assumed all mountains did that. I

was always looking for the shape of a face, the dip of waist and legs. This one does it best.

Okay, I was really running late now.

I jumped back into the Prius and kept going, off the Huon Highway and into the deep green slopes and dips of Grove. Mountains, river, houses and paddocks. I had a parcel to deliver.

I'd been to this farm before. I didn't realise that until I was almost there. I was following the GPS directions for 'Farmstay Cottages' but when I pulled up at the spot, there were no cottages in sight. Instead, there was a long, narrow dirt road disappearing up into a bushy incline, and a hand-painted sign on the cast-iron letterbox that said Wee Goat Farm.

There was another, larger sign on one of the paddocks on either side of the dirt track, proclaiming that The Third Annual Big Wee Goat Race would be held there on the first Sunday of February.

I hadn't driven myself, when I visited last year. I'd been part of a grand promenade for a professional photo shoot, involving green wedding dresses, fluttering veils, barefoot fashion models, and several tiny goats. That had been an odd day.

Still, I wasn't going to get this package delivered unless I stopped daydreaming and found someone to ask for directions. Rural properties laugh in the face of GPS pins and map apps. So often, it says you've arrived when actually you're further away than you were when you started. Or you're on the wrong side of a massive acreage, and the only way to get there from here is to go back to where you started and try again.

Advances in technology aren't always cut out for the country.

I set off valiantly up the rattling dirt road that could only be called a driveway with a great generosity of imagination. Before I got very far, I met a battered ute coming the other way. The driver slowed, both of us pulling over to the side. There was almost enough space for him to edge past, but I was a hair away from tipping into a ditch.

We both wound our windows down to speak to each other, raising our voices to be heard over the very noisy border collie in the flat tray of his ute, who definitely thought her contribution to the conversation was more important than anything either of us stupid humans had to say.

"Are you lost?" he asked, wary at first, before recognition dawned. "We've met."

Ah, one of the goat farming brothers. This one, who I had mentally christened Arms in Flannel last time we met, was what they had in mind when the phrase 'ruggedly handsome' entered the vocabulary of romance authors. He had a stalk of hay in his rumpled hair. Be still, my heaving bosom.

"I have a parcel to deliver to the Farmstay Cottages," I called over to him. "Is that here?"

"Yeah, up behind the house. Did our sign fall off again?"

"I only saw the goat sign."

"That'd be right. I told Bry to fix that bloody nail. Belfry, Love Shack or Man Cave?"

I blinked at him. "I'm pretty sure none of those are star signs."

He laughed a little, without opening his mouth, so all the work was done by his shoulders. It was quite a sight. Lots of flannel straining over muscles. So outdoorsy. "Those are the cottage names."

"Oh. I checked the parcel. "All I have on this one is P. West, Farmstay Cottages." The customer had requested I leave it at the door, but I have to admit, I was curious to meet her in person.

"The Belfry," he said. "Chuck it over to me, if you like. I can take it to our guest later. She's here for another month. Writing novels, I think? Brought her own typewriter."

"An actual typewriter?" That was impressively retro. "Well, now she has her own vintage frock to type in." Convenience beat curiosity. I passed over the parcel, which was wrapped in brown paper and tied up in string because Paisley insists that our customers like the old school personal touch. A customer with her own typewriter would probably appreciate that sort of thing. "Cheers for that, is there somewhere I can turn around?"

"Just over the rise of the hill. Keep an eye out for goats." He gave me searching look, like he was still trying to place me. "Green dress, is it?"

"Not this time. It's bright red!" I smiled, though, to show him he was on the right track.

"You don't have any more of those fashion shoots coming, do you? The magazine paid us eventually, but they left the valley in a hell of a mess."

He paused, leaving me wondering if he remembered all the other stuff that happened last year, the murder and such. Far from Wee Goat Farm, but they must have heard about it. It was heavily covered in the media, and even more heavily whispered about in the local gossip network. Nothing stays quiet long when you live on an island.

There had even been a high profile interview with me that I really wished I hadn't agreed to — like I needed more strangers to be able to recognise me in the street — but there was no putting that horse back in the barn now.

Today at least, this particular bloke didn't feel the need to interrogate me about my past. Instead, he gazed broodingly into the distance like he was posing for the cover of Hot Farmer Monthly, Ute Edition. "See you around." A man of few words.

"Hope your visitor likes her dress," I offered brightly.

And that was it. Arms in Flannel drove off. I kept chugging up the hill until I could turn around and make my way out of the narrow dirt driveway, to the dulcet barking noise of a second border collie on the veranda.

A basic exchange. The story should have ended there.

I didn't think about Wee Goat Farm or their Farmstay Cottages again, until a few days later: when the news began reporting the mysterious death of a woman wearing the same bright red dress.

～

"I'm beginning to think no one actually understands what a fashion detective is," complained Paisley.

"Do you know?" I shot back.

"I thought I did."

Paisley is ten years younger than me: twenty years old, non-binary (pronouns: they/them) and casually fabulous in a way I always find faintly intimidating. It was their idea to start up as fashion detectives after our one modest success at solving a crime. I guess kids today are used the idea of inventing their own jobs.

Today, Paisley was wearing a satin dinner jacket printed with skulls over a black t-shirt and cargo shorts. Summer-wear for the young and glam.

We were sitting on the back deck of my sister Trace's tiny house at Kingston Beach. Technically my home too, as I've been renting a room here for more than a year now.

It doesn't feel like mine; it doesn't even really feel like Trace's. Everything about it, from the five zillion throw cushions and crocheted antimacassars, all the way through to the antique china teacup and half-finished cryptic crossword books, belongs to Aunt Harriet, Trace's ex-husband's great-aunt (deceased).

We haven't done much to put our own stamp on the place since Trace's divorce went through and the property became legally hers. That could change very soon, because Trace decided this was the month to let her daughter Daisy finally have a puppy. A tiny, yappy, maybe-part-terrier dog rescue, currently chasing Trace and Dais around the postage stamp-sized back yard.

Aunt Harriet's deck is tiny too: there's barely room for

a patio set (2 chairs, 1 round table, both looking like they have been crocheted out of wrought iron) and a few potted herbs. On this particular day, Paisley and I took over the patio set with big glasses of strawberry mint iced tea, since the others were busy romping.

Technically, this was a business meeting. Though I wasn't convinced we actually had a business venture to speak of. It's one thing to stick up a notice in the window of Fashionably Late, the upcycled fashion boutique where we both work:

The Fashion Detectives
We Solve Crimes Connected To Clothing,
Costumes and Couture
Reasonable Rates, Inquire Within.

But when it came to the work we were being offered, well... The customers had a very different idea of what being a fashion detective entailed than what Paisley had first envisaged. They were feeling a bit grumpy about the whole thing.

Trace left Daisy and the new pup for a few minutes, and came over to claim her own glass of tea. "I thought you'd had a bunch of enquiries," she said, wiping a line of sweat from under her curly hair. It was one of those rare Tasmanian summer days where the Antarctic breezes don't actually sweep in from the south to cool things down by 4pm. We'd eaten dinner already, and the house felt like an oven.

"Sure," said Paisley, tapping their painted Blundstone

boots against the stem of the patio table. "But I was thinking actual *crimes* involving fashion. Not sourcing rare Bolivian buttons on eBay to match a specific vintage blouse. Or tracking down a box of old shoes they didn't mean to give away to Vinnies…"

"There was the Case of the Stolen Tweed Jackets," I said, reminding Paisley of my own recent triumph.

Paisley rolled their eyes. "Except the owner didn't know they'd been taken until we knocked on his door, didn't mind at all that they'd been turned into handbags, and promptly donated them to the thieves on the grounds that it was nice to see young people with a 'thriving entrepreneurial spirit' in the community."

"Happy endings all around," I agreed.

"Ugh!"

"I'm not sure what the problem is," said Trace. "Daisy, no, don't drag the stick off him! Wait for him to drop it! You two are really good at these sorts of jobs. Tracking down rare fashion items. It's your skillset."

"True," said Paisley, and we clinked glasses. "It's just… how is that different from our actual job at Fashionably Late? Like our last case — we were asked to find a replica of a famous evening dress with a matching scarf. We found something similar enough, Sam here dyed it, I did the alterations. Sam delivered the dress. That is literally a Fashionably Late commission, not a detective job. No crime in sight."

"I mean, I don't mind our mysteries being gentle and clothing-related," I put in. "I like my job! And the customer was happy to pay extra for the research time. Morgaine doesn't mind us taking on our own jobs that use the resources of the shop, because she's the most laidback boss ever."

"I know," sighed Paisley. "Just, that whole thing last year was really exciting, you know."

Trace and I exchanged glances. Yep, a fashion-related murder case was very exciting. Also terrifying, and not the sort of thing likely to come up every day. Me, I was more than happy to stick to the mysteries involving button hunts and custom dye jobs.

Leave the murder to the professionals.

Daisy, nine years old and clearly never going to love any of us as much as she loved her new puppy Demi, let out a short scream. We all looked up in alarm, but no. Scream of excitement. As you were.

"It wasn't a red evening dress, was it?" Trace asked in a wondering sort of voice.

I held my hands up. You could still see the red under my fingernails — I use gloves for all dyeing work, obviously, but I'd still got caught when tidying things away. Sneaky stuff, dye. It had left me rocking the sloppy serial killer aesthetic, which explained the weird looks I'd got in the post office. "Red as the Queen of Hearts."

"And when you say famous…"

"That was why this one sounded so promising," moaned Pais. "You know the Prue Scythe story from like, a million years ago? The filmmaker who disappeared at the Diabolique Film Festival."

"Fifteen years ago," I corrected with all the patience of someone with more than a decade of adulthood under her belt.

"Sure, whatever. All very mysterious. Was she

murdered? Was she abducted? Why does someone need an exact copy of her dress? But you just know it's gonna turn out the customer wanted it for some 'unsolved crime' theme party. No legit mystery in sight."

"That's a good thing," I insisted. "Our customer paid top dollar for that job. If your fashion detective sign brings in that kind of work, and we don't end up running away from surprise murderers, that's a positive outcome."

"You sound like Morgaine," Paisley grumped.

Trace was looking twitchy. "Are you saying *you* made a replica of the dress Prue Scythe was wearing when she disappeared," she said, bright eyed. "Right? The red vintage dress with the scarf?"

We both blinked at her, like idiots.

"Why?" I asked my sister.

"Because," said Trace. "Isaac couldn't come over tonight because there's been a local death he had to investigate today, down at Grove, and the media has gone into overdrive about it. And then I read some news articles — I figured it had to be the same case."

"What case?" I demanded.

Paisley was already on their phone, searching. "Whoa," they said. "I don't believe it. That's our frock. *The* frock."

"They found Prue Scythe this morning," Trace said quietly. "Here, in Tasmania, on some farm. Dead. And according to the news report I saw…"

"She was wearing the same dress as when she disappeared," said Paisley, reading off their phone. "Or… one that looked exactly like it. Red vintage. An exact replica."

Our dress. Oh, bloody hell.

"Buttons," I complained, already stabbing at my own phone to see what they were talking about. "I really *like* hunting rare Bolivian buttons. They're so restful, and almost never lead to some of us having to make statements to the police."

2

INSPECTOR ROSENTHAL AND I HAVE HISTORY, YOU
might say.

On the one hand, he's the detective who arrested me
for fraud a few years ago. He's not technically the person
who wrecked my old life (I reserve that honour for my ex-
husband, the true culprit of the fraud, who put more effort
into framing me than he ever did into our marriage), but
Rosenthal didn't cover himself in glory, either.

I'd have happily never set eyes on him again, except…
except I kind of ended up helping him on a case last year,
and now he's dating my sister.

Rosenthal is not just the detective inspector whose
actions left me with a strong anxiety trigger around any
kind of interaction with the police… he's also Isaac, who
remembers Daisy's favourite flavour of ice cream, and
makes Trace smile.

Yep, it's awkward. Super awkward. But in this family,
we don't shy away from awkward. We suck it up, and
invite awkward to dinner. Sometimes, we even invite

awkward over after dinner to explain our involvement in another fashion-related murder.

Fun times.

"This dress?" Rosenthal asked, pushing a crime scene photo across the kitchen table towards me.

It was taken at a careful angle, so you could see as much of the dress as possible without any identifying parts of the person wearing the dress, though from the colour of the skin under the asymmetrical frothy red sleeve… yeah, I would never mistake this for a photo of an alive person.

"This dress," I confirmed heavily.

We were in the kitchen now. Night was falling properly, which happens about 9pm at the height of a Tasmanian summer. Daisy was in bed, having been tearfully separated from Demi the puppy, also thankfully asleep. Trace was standing guard in the hallway to make sure Daisy didn't interrupt our serious adult conversation… and also to make sure she could discreetly eavesdrop on everything we said without looking like she was being nosy. (It's a very small house.)

Paisley and I were officially helping the police with their enquiries. Sergeant Deng was here for formality's sake, though he had accepted a sparkling water and was leaning against the kitchen bench, not involving himself in the conversation.

The electric fan was going full-bore, mostly moving the warm air around instead of cooling things down. The back door opened out of the kitchen, with a fly screen door closed to keep mozzies and flies from making our lives truly miserable.

We were going to have to think about getting some air

conditioning in this house, if the summers continued to get hotter. I wondered how Aunt Harriet would feel about that. Presumably if she was still hanging around to haunt us, we wouldn't feel the heat.

Inspector Rosenthal looked tense. There was a particular crease between his eyes that he only got when his personal life mixed with a murder case. This was the second time I'd ever seen it.

"So," he said, opening his old school notebook. "You don't know who ordered the dress?"

"We didn't meet them," Paisley corrected. "Someone called P West ordered it by email. That was the name on the credit card payment too, I checked."

"Can you print those emails out for me?" he asked.

Paisley looked startled at the very idea someone might bother print out an email.

"We absolutely can," I told him. "Um. Tomorrow?" Trace didn't have a printer in the house, but there was one at the shop.

"And you delivered the dress?" Rosenthal asked, looking directly at me.

I immediately felt guilty. It was our thing, his and mine. He asked questions, I felt waves of guilt and paranoia, and then afterwards I discussed it all in great detail with my therapist. "Why do you assume it was me?"

"Reese Carmichael, co-owner of Wee Goat Farm, mentioned that the only visitor our deceased received this week was a cute dressmaker in a Prius, dropping off a parcel two days before she died." Rosenthal's careful tone made it very clear that this was a direct quote.

"I'm cute," said Paisley, pretending to be offended.

"You don't drive," I reminded them. I gave Rosenthal what had to be a very bright smile. "He said I was cute?" I'm in my thirties, and surrounded all day by customers who are younger, brighter and more fashion forward than I'll ever be. I'll take cute from a hot farmer in flannel any day of the week.

Rosenthal's blandest ever facial expression gave me no further information.

Trace popped her head in from the hallway. "No flirting with murder suspects, Sam," she reminded me.

Honestly, that happened *one time*.

"He's not a murder suspect," I said immediately, then looked to Inspector Rosenthal. "Wait, is Reese Carmichael a murder suspect?"

Surely miniature goat farmers were presented with get-out-of-jail free cards simply for making the world more wholesome?

"This is you helping us with our enquiries," Rosenthal said tiredly. "Not the other way around. And I agree with Tracy that you should wait until after the investigation is concluded before you flirt with anyone. Based on past experience."

I was feeling so attacked right now.

"Did you know about the Prue Scythe abduction when you made the dress?" Rosenthal continued, back to business.

"I mean, I had to Google her," Paisley admitted.

Trace and I made identical outraged scoffing sounds. Some of us didn't have to Google it, okay? Some of us were there when the story was all over the news. Fashion, mystery, glamour. Prue Scythe was an icon for our generation.

Okay, I'd had to check online photo references for the dress, but I still remembered the basic details.

Our reaction made Rosenthal's mouth turn up slightly in a smile. He was Isaac again. "Okay," he said, making himself as comfortable as possible in Aunt Harriet's squeakiest kitchen chair. "Tell me the Prue Scythe story."

I was sixteen when Prue Scythe vanished. I already knew who she was. I don't think there's a single Australian teenager at the time who hadn't heard of her.

The first Vamp Pash movie was a quirky indie film, about a busload of teenagers who get stranded in the outback after their bus driver is killed by a vampire. It went… well, viral isn't the word for it. It went international, in a way that low budget Australian films rarely do. The YA book series it was based on, written by the improbably-named author Vanity Fall, became best-sellers.

By the time Vamp Pash II rolled around, we were ready for it. The date movie of the summer. Every Australian teenager either loved or hated Vamp Pash II, and whether you got dragged along to watch it by an obsessed friend or you hate-watched it with a giant box of popcorn… you had to see it. You couldn't avoid it.

The six main co-stars (former soap stars, now super world famous) went from grungey first movie indie actors to glamorous and shiny stars, appearing on every magazine cover, falling in love with each other and announcing massive new movie deals every other week. Some of them even made it to America. The ones who didn't still get invited to do panto in the UK ever year. Yes. That's how famous they were.

Vamp Pash II ended with a post-credits cliffhanger, with no one knowing if Marnie would choose to be with Cedric or Carmilla. The internet filled up with angsty fanfic and desperate head canons. We were promised a third movie. There had to be a third movie.

(Even those who claimed to hate vampire movies all had Opinions about Marnie and her romantic choices.)

Prue Scythe was the director of the first two Vamp Pash movies. There were rumours that the studio wanted to replace her for the third, bring in someone more experi-enced (male) and established (American). But Prue had built her own following, and the fans adored her. Social media was still in its early days then — Facebook and Youtube were just getting started — but Prue had a Vamp Pash blog that had chronicled the making of the first two films. She put up exclusive behind the scenes content.

Prue would have been all over Insta and Twitter, if we had them back then. Her look was iconic: black bobbed hair, bright red lipstick, giant sunglasses. A scythe tattoo on her left arm. A British accent so posh that she could have been one of Bridget Jones' BFFs. She was old, of course — we were young enough that mid-to-late thirties seemed old — but she was *cool*.

There were rumours that Vanity Fall, the author of the books, refused to sign a deal for a third film unless Prue was attached. The fans agreed, loudly.

Then came the Diabolique film festival in Sydney. It

had been nearly a year since Vamp Pash II came out, and Prue teased an announcement at the festival on her blog. Would she show new footage? Announce which actors/characters were coming back? Would we get a release date?

The last time anyone saw Prue Scythe alive was at the opening of the festival, wearing a glamorous asymmetrical red gown (the scythe tattoo visible underneath the frothy left sleeve), her goth makeup perfect.

We saw that footage a lot, because after she disappeared from her hotel room later that night, the news played it over and over. At first it was pitched as a 'diva director disappoints fans' story. Then it became a missing persons case, and then a celebrity murder enquiry, before finally settling into being a Famous Unsolved Mystery.

The whole story got an extra flutter when it leaked that Prue Scythe was a fake name all along: she'd been born Lady Prudence Sotheby in jolly old England, and ran away in her teens. No one back home had seen her for years until she popped up in Australia as a cult film director.

This gave the media new photos to print at least — pics of her as a fat toddler, posing in unflattering dresses and hair bows, and a few awkward, blurry snaps of Prudence at boarding school with friends.

There was no Vamp Pash III. The sixth book in the series was quietly published a few months later, and then Vanity Fall stopped writing. There was a popular fan theory, never confirmed publicly by the publisher, that Prue Scythe had been Vanity Fall all along. Why have two names when you could have three?

What really happened to Prue Scythe when she disappeared? No one ever found out.

Until, apparently, she turned up dead on a goat farm in rural Tasmania, fifteen years later.

"So," said Paisley. "Did you ship Marnie with Cedric or Carmilla?"

"Marnie was the worst," Trace said, popping in from the hallway. "Cedric and Carmilla belonged together."

"I always thought Vincent deserved a decent love interest," I said wistfully.

"You would," she said, rolling her eyes. "Sam, you have the worst taste in men. Vincent ate people."

"Not in the books!"

"Ugh, you and those books. I still remember when you said book!Cedric and film!Marnie were your OTP and anyone who thought otherwise could eat dirt."

"I was only up to Book 3 when I said that! Book!Cedric went way downhill. Too clingy."

Rosenthal cleared his throat. "Do you know of any connection between your customer, P West, and Prue Scythe?"

"No idea," I admitted. "She — I assume she's a she — asked us to recreate the dress from the classic news photos. We didn't get into deep discussions about, you know. The celebrity angle. I don't think she even mentioned Prue Scythe. But I recognised the dress from the photos. We assumed it was for a party. Or cosplayers. Except cosplayers usually agree to have formal fittings, they know the value of doing things properly. P West didn't want to come to the shop in person, and she insisted on contactless delivery."

I had been a bit cheeky, hoping to sneak a peek by delivering the parcel in person — if it hadn't been from the distracting handsomeness of the very helpful Reese Carmichael, I might have got a look at our mysterious customer!

I saw Rosenthal write the word 'cosplayers' down very carefully.

"Cosplayers over the years had done a lot of the work for us, to be honest," Paisley put in. "Some of the shaping of the dress was unusual — that frothy effect on the shoulder and hem — but we didn't have to come up with a design from scratch. We sourced a similar dress to use as the base, and then…"

"Was there a scarf?" Rosenthal asked. "The original footage shows a long red scarf, but it wasn't with the body. Hasn't been found on the property — we conducted a second search today."

"Yes," I said quickly. "We had to make that from scratch. It was in the parcel."

I'd made it myself, actually. Paisley and Morgaine decided recently that I can be trusted with straight-line sewing that isn't too complicated — so scarves, basically. The occasional A-line skirt if we're all feeling brave.

"Perfectly colour matched," Paisley added. "Not easy when the thread count of the fabric was so much heavier than…"

I cut in before they got more technical than Rosenthal needed from us. "Are you sure the dead woman at the farm is the real Prue Scythe? No one's seen her in fifteen years. If it's just some woman who looks like her in that dress, then cosplayer is more likely. An obsessed fan, you know."

"When did she die?" Paisley added, ghoulishly fascinated. "Like, how long ago? Was her body on the farm all this time? Did someone dig her up to dress up a skeleton in the dress we made?"

I shuddered at that thought. Vampire movies were at my limit of gross-out content... I hadn't even been able to re-watch the first Vamp Pash movie in recent years. Too much gore, not enough smooching.

"She died three days ago," Inspector Rosenthal said heavily. "I wasn't brought in until today, but the local investigating team got the DNA testing fast tracked because someone on the scene gave us a tip this was connected to the Scythe case. It had been leaked to the press, too. It's amazing how fast the labs manage to produce results when a story hits the media. We've identified the dead woman as Lady Prudence Sotheby, known professionally as Prue Scythe. She booked into Farmstay Cottages at Wee Goat Farm under the name Pamela West, earlier this month."

We all looked at him, impatient to learn more.

"And?" Trace asked, finally.

Her boyfriend closed his notebook. "And it's an ongoing investigation. So I shouldn't tell you any more than I already have."

We all let out groans.

"But where has she been the last fifteen years?" Paisley whined. "Surely that's at least as interesting as who killed her now."

"I'll let you know if I have any more dress-related questions," said Inspector Rosenthal, back to business. "Samantha, I'd appreciate those printouts of any correspondence you had with Ms West, email or otherwise. And photographs, if you have them, of the garments the two of you made. We'll need to keep an eye out for that scarf."

He didn't warn me, Paisley or Trace that we should refrain from investigating the mystery on our own. He probably thought that went without saying.

Bless.

3

"WE'VE GOT A CASE!" PAISLEY ANNOUNCED, THE following day. I was half an hour away from finishing my shift at Fashionably Late, the upcycled fashion boutique where we work. I was hanging laundry on one of the several Hills Hoist washing lines in the back yard behind the shop when Paisley pounced.

(An upcycled fashion boutique requires a lot of sewing, mending and altering skills, which everyone else around here has in spades, plus fetching, carrying, washing and dyeing, which mostly fall to me. It's the most relaxing job I've ever had.)

"A fashion detective client?" I asked, just to be sure.

"Yes!"

"And that means you'll stop obsessing about the Prue Scythe case now?" I was a little concerned at how deeply Paisley had fallen down the rabbit hole of web research on this one. I was pretty sure they'd spent the last two hours searching for 'where are they now' stories about the Vamp Pash stars.

"Haha harr," said Paisley, with the manic energy of a very young person who lives mostly on caffeine and Wi-Fi. "That's the best bit. This *is* the Prue Scythe case."

Today, they were dressed in an aesthetic could best be described as Pirate at Their First Rave: a floofy white shirt and a red sequined sash over a black scort and plaid socks.

"Paisley, no," I sighed.

"Paisley, *yes*."

"Rosenthal's going to bake me in an *oven*."

"Nah, he wants to stay on your good side to keep Trace happy. C'mon, Sam. One visit to Wee Goat Farms to meet our client. Aren't you even a teeny bit curious?"

"And also, you need me to drive," I muttered.

It wasn't like I was going to let Paisley go running off to play detective, fashion or otherwise, without me… but I had to put up at least token resistance, as the only one of us who has been a grown up for more than ten minutes.

"I do need you to drive," Paisley reassured me. "But don't think that's all you bring to the party. I also respect your powerful crone-like wisdom and your ability to use the map function on your phone."

Sweet. "Did you at least ask Morgaine about the car?"

Paisley did a shimmy. "Trace says we can take hers! As long as we fill her in on everything later."

Right, then. "Better help me hang out the rest of this washing so I can leave on time. And then you can explain everything on the way. Leave nothing out."

I did not want to walk into whatever situation Paisley had set up for us without knowing exactly what was going on.

This was my first time inside the main farmhouse of Wee Goat Farm. It did not disappoint. It had a real log-cabin feel, bright and open, with the biggest Huon Pine kitchen table I had ever seen. Warm, inviting: the kind of rustic you see on Instagram, rather than real life.

There was an ancient pine dresser (that classic piece of Australian kitchen furniture) that had been lovingly restored. The table was basically a giant slice of tree, highly polished. The kitchen floor was old slate. The teacups were mismatched, vintage and porcelain.

The two gorgeous border collies, who had barked furiously at us when we rolled up to park on the gravel driveway, were now lolling around on the kitchen floor asking for belly rubs.

Oh, and there were the Carmichael brothers: Reese, the smouldering one I'd previously met a couple of times, and Bryson (call me Bry), his ball-of-sunshine brother. Between them, they ran the goat farm and the farmstay cottages — and had time, apparently to renovate their own furniture, chop their own wood, and sweep their own floor.

Forgive me if I swoon.

"We host breakfasts down here for the guests," said Bry, bouncing on his heels as he poured the tea. "Sometimes the guests who choose the cottages for bushland solitude don't take us up on the offer, but once they've tasted Reese's omelettes, you can't keep them away."

"Yeah yeah," said Reese, rolling his eyes. "These two aren't here to review us on Yelp, mate."

I was surrounded by attractive farmers in flannel, and

apparently at least one of them could cook. I might have to move in.

"I'm not sure exactly what we are here for," I said, producing my best friendly and unthreatening vibe. It usually puts people at ease. I think it actually made Reese more edgy. "Paisley said you want to hire us, but now there's a police investigation underway, there isn't a lot we can contribute."

"I agree," said Reese immediately. "This is a terrible idea, and we're all wasting our time."

Well, all right then.

"You promised to give this a shot," his brother argued.

"It's a stupid idea, Bry."

They glared at each other. The warm sunshine in the room ebbed, ever so slightly.

Then Bry turned back to us, his friendly smile pasted back on with only a hint less bounce than before. "The thing is, the police are barking up the wrong tree."

Reese rolled his eyes. "Because this one can't have a conversation with any woman under… sixty, apparently, without flirting up a storm."

"That's not relevant to the situation," Bry said, still smiling. "Though I'll admit Inspector Murphy seems to think I'm hiding something about my perfectly platonic interactions with Pam West."

"Didn't really help that you flirted with Inspector Murphy, too." Reese sighed.

"Briefly. I don't flirt where I'm not wanted!"

"So the police suspect you of being involved with the murder?" I asked carefully.

"I know!" said Bry, as if this was the most ridiculous notion anyone could have ever come up with. "*Me*."

"They're just doing their job," Reese argued. "They have to suspect everyone."

Mmm, yes. Doing their job. I'd heard that before. Sometimes doing their job meant arresting innocent people and ruining their lives.

"Here's the thing," said Bry. "Inspector Murphy was fine with me — routine, neutral. But then after she spoke to the guests, she came back at me, all aggressive, insisting I was hiding some sort of relationship with Pam."

"You mean Prue?" I asked.

He shrugged. "We knew her as Pam."

I looked from one brother to the other. Reese was tense. Bry was, now I came to pay attention, a little too all smiles, like there was panic behind his warm hazel eyes.

"What is it you think the police were told?" I asked.

"We don't know," Reese said impatiently. "But they keep coming *back*. They've searched the bush around the cottages all the way down towards the creek three times already. Normally I'd be the first to say Bry was paranoid. But this Inspector Murphy definitely has it in for him. Which does not mean we need to start hiring amateur detectives," he added sternly.

"That's what the rainy day fund is for, Reese!"

"It really isn't."

"Mum agrees with me."

"Mum always agrees with you, that's why I keep getting outvoted when it comes to crazy business decisions. Do you have any idea how stressful it is to be the only logical person in this family?"

Rosenthal was right. I shouldn't be involved in this, and I shouldn't immediately assume that attractive men with nice shoulders were innocent. I'd learned that one the hard way.

I gave Paisley a Look. They rolled their eyes at me.

"Thing is," Bry said reasonably, in the tones of someone who was good looking, and a younger sibling, and was used to getting his own way. "We're not expecting you to like, unmask the killer. But right now we have three guests up in those cottages, and at least one of them not only made the police think I'm some kind of maniac, they also blabbed to the journos. That's assuming none of them are actually, you know…"

"The murderer," Reese said grimly.

"Well, yeah," said Bry. "Exactly! We need to get this wrapped up fast, before it affects our business more than it already has. Bad enough the media is trying to turn this into a huge story." Right on cue, I heard a helicopter go overhead. Could the network news channels not afford drones these days?

"This is a small community," said Reese. "Farmers, small business owners. We help each other out. If rumours start flying around about my brother being a murderer…" He looked at Bry. "We should cancel the Wee Goat Race. We can't afford another disaster."

"Cancelling would be a disaster," Bry argued back. "It would be like admitting we did the murder!"

"Nobody would think that!"

Bry gave me the widest-eyed look imaginable. He did not, it had to be said, look at all like a murderer.

"What are your expectations here?" I asked cautiously. "For the Fashion Detectives."

Reese winced as if the very phrase 'fashion detectives' was giving him a headache.

"Okay!" said Bry, grinning with manic delight. "So what I'm thinking is, you two stick around for afternoon tea, eat some delicious scones with homemade jam, and see what vibes you get from our guests. If you can figure out the whole murder business before the police arrest me *for no reason*, that would be great."

I was curious. Of course I was. This little side venture would give me the opportunity to find out more about the whole Prue Scythe business. I wasn't getting a dishonest vibe from the brothers, but they had to know more than they were saying. Reese in particular kept darting Bry looks like he couldn't believe what was coming out of his mouth.

Also, I did enjoy like scones with jam. "Apart from the dress she was wearing," I mused. "It doesn't really sound like a fashion mystery. Does it, Paisley?"

"You are the only detectives we know about locally," said Bry, widening his eyes. You know how they say pets often look like their owners? This man was border collie, all the way through. "Our mum is friends with Diana Wave, she recommended you."

Oh, that made things… slightly more difficult. Diana ruled all our lives at Fashionably Late. If she wanted us to investigate, we probably should.

"I am happy to mend any flannel shirts that need darning while eating delicious homemade scones," Paisley offered. "Just to make it all a little more fashion-relevant."

I looked at the china teacup Bry had our before me. It had a pattern of cornflowers on it. Adorable.

"Okay," I said, trying not to look too enthusiastic. "We'll meet the suspects. But maybe first you could show us, you know?"

Paisley knew what I was getting at. "The scene of the crime."

"Before more police turn up to kick us out," I added. It wasn't unlikely. If Rosenthal caught me and Paisley snooping around, he'd ban us from the property in a shot. Maybe we should have brought Trace with us. He has way more trouble saying no to her…

"I'll do it," said Bry, getting to his feet. "Happy to show you everything. Chug your tea or bring it with you. Reese —"

"Yeah, yeah," said his brother, already reaching for a bag of flour. "I'll bake the bloody scones."

The thing about being a detective, even a not very official one who mostly deals in buttons, is I really love being a detective. Figuring out problems and pulling threads until you get to the other end of a really tricky bit is my favourite thing to do. When I ran my own business, I was constantly troubleshooting, putting out fires and pulling off miracles.

Working for Fashionably Late had been exactly the right little no-stress basic job I needed after all my personal drama a couple of years ago. But now? Since the new work started trickling in, drawn by Paisley's Fashion

Detectives sign, I've been more… well. Challenged.
Sparked up. Alive.

It's also possible that after that one time I accidentally
solved a murder, I started reading vintage crime novels by
the armful. Just to, you know. Keep my hand in. In case
the opportunity comes up again.

Here it was now, wrapped up in a gown I'd dyed
myself, and a vampire franchise I'd loved as a teenager.

Given the opportunity to see where on the farm Prue
Scythe/Lady Prudence Whatsisface had met her untimely
end, I was all for it. Part of me knew I wasn't going to
have that kind of amazing luck again, to be able to pull all
the pieces together, solve it before it became blindingly
obvious I had trusted the wrong person.

But part of me really wanted this to be a thing I was
good at.

"Don't mind Reese, he's always been a bit of a
grouch," Bry said as we followed the dirt road up the hill,
away from the farm. "Also, he found Pam's body. He's
still a bit shaken up by it all."

The dogs followed us up the hill, happy enough to get
a run at this end of the day. Not that they lacked for exer-
cise on a property like this.

"You would be, too," I said. My own first brush with a
dead body had been too close to home. I still can't put on a
load of laundry without thinking about everything that
went down last year. "That's normal."

"Yeah, I suppose. I did flirt with her," Bry added. "I
mean, she was nice. The older ladies like it, a bit of a smile
and a chat. They always review us well. I wasn't inappro-
priate or anything."

I'd been reading a lot about murder — the real kind as well as the fictional — on my days off. Research, research, research. "They're looking for a partner," I told him. "That's standard with murdered women. Because, you know. Crime stats."

"Yeah, no, I get it," he agreed. "And there's the dogs."

"The dogs?"

We could see the cottages as we walked up the hill — the dirt driveway branched off three times, leading to three sweet-looking chalet style houses. Each had a brightly painted sign out front. The Man Cave, decorated with... not sure. Some sort of chicken leg? No, it was grey. A stone club! There was a swish looking hire car parked in front.

Then the Love Shack, with hearts painted all over the sign, in retro lettering. This cottage had a big, seen-better-days white van parked in front, with the words Archer's Dry Cleaning professionally painted on the side.

Finally, at the crest of the hill: The Belfry, with a few cute, lopsided cartoon bats. No car in sight.

"You heard them when you drove up," said Bry. "Walking, driving... no one can come up that road past the main house without Bandit and Chilli going nuts. They were quiet the night that Pam was murdered. All night. Not a peep out of them. Reese found her early, when he and the dogs came up here for a walk. About 6 AM. Wearing that whole — you know." He mimed the red dress with which I was very familiar, including the frothy tulle over-the-shoulder effect.

Past the Belfry now, and with no more dirt road, we were looking down the other side of the slope. It was all grass and trees, heading down towards a wide, dry-as-a-bone creek.

The Huon Valley is famous for staying green and damp, even at the height of a Tasmanian summer, but it's not literally magic. By February, even the wettest waterways start getting thirsty.

"She was down there," Bry said, pointing. "On this side of the bank."

It was chilling to think of a real human person lying dead on the ground down there, wearing a dress I'd worked on. I'd agonised over getting the shade of scarlet perfect, only for the dress to end up cut to bits in a morgue somewhere.

Pam West — Lady Prudence — Prue Scythe had died two days after I delivered the gown. I wished now that I'd handed it over personally, and not only because I really loved her films when I was young. It probably wouldn't have made a difference to whether she lived or died, but it felt so weird that I'd never met her face to face.

Perhaps if I had, I'd feel worse right now.

Bandit and Chilli were way ahead of us, running back and forth. The humans walked more slowly.

"This isn't quite where we did that film shoot last year, is it?" I said, trying to orient myself. I remembered a fairy bower, and a babbling brook…

"Nah, that's around the curve of the creek," Bry said, pointing down river. "It's narrower there."

"Could anyone have walked up from that direction, accessed the property that way?"

"I mean, sure, if they hopped about three electric fences and walked about 4ks through the bush, in the dark.

But the police seem pretty certain no one did. Inspector Murphy was very emphatic about it. The only suspects they're looking at are me, Reese, and the three guests."

"Any neighbours in the other direction?"

"Two or three sets of electric fences everywhere except the shared fence line with the alpaca farm over the hill," said Bry. "And security cams everywhere. The Inspector already secured all the footage. Up that way — once you get past the creek and a whole lot of acres of bush, you'll eventually hit a daffodil farm. Which also has security cams and electric fences." He shook his head, eyes drawn back to a particular flat piece of rock that had Bandit and Chilli very interested indeed. "Nah. Someone would have to pull of some kind of James Bond bullshit to get all the way up here and away again without being seen, or leaving any trace. The way the police looked over this place on the first day, there wasn't a gumboot track unaccounted for. They spent like, a day and a half staring at the creek bed, looking for footprints."

"So," said Paisley. "It's one of you five, then? Most likely."

"Looks like it," said Bry. He looked back at me. "Police say we all have to stay in residence on the property until the investigation's over. We can't kick them out. Now, I *know* Reese didn't do anything to the nice type-writer lady. And he knows I didn't do anything to her. That leaves three suspects. All stuck here in *our* farmstay cottages until the police decide which one did the murder. Their bookings run out in a few days, so we're going to have to cancel other guests to keep them here. Unless someone figures out who killed Pam."

Bry was still looking at me. Expectantly.

No pressure, then.

"I'll see what I can do," I agreed. "But in the mean-time, it wouldn't hurt to have a good lawyer on standby."

What I didn't say was, that would probably be a much better investment for their Rainy Day fund.

4

FROM OUTSIDE, THE FARMHOUSE LOOKED LIKE SOMETHING off a postcard, especially in the late afternoon summer sunshine with all the greenery of the gum trees around us. It had a verandah wide enough to host a quilting party or two, and the very modern touch of a wheelchair ramp on one side.

Rustic, but up to date. Nothing felt new, but there was a lovingly restored feeling about the place.

"Is it just the two of you living here?" I asked Bry as we headed back. The house was big enough for a massive intergenerational family.

They'd mentioned their mother, but I saw no sign of another person around.

"Just us," he said. "And the goats."

~

If you are the kind of person who thinks that goats are adorable, and I recognise that they're not for everyone, then let me tell you something about miniature goats: they are JUST. SO. CUTE. Big eyes, floppy ears, tiny everything.

They're also a little scary. Like toddlers. Big eyes, the ability to defeat adults in single combat, and wow can they eat.

I'm not saying that if you ever needed to hide a body, a team of miniature goats would get that done for you in under an hour. But also, I'm not *not* saying that.

While Paisley and I were stickybeaking the scene of the crime with Bry, Reese had been making magic with his hands in a bowl of flour. The best thing about scones is how quick they are to make. The second best thing is when someone else makes them for you. No, wait. Those two facts are the wrong way around.

"Who's in which cottage?" I asked when we returned to the hot kitchen with the good baking smells.

Two miniature goats had refused to return to the paddock when Bry asked them nicely, so followed him in when we returned to the kitchen. Paisley was now sitting cross-legged on the slate tiles, delighted with a lapful of love. "Something about love shacks and man caves?" they suggested. "Would the plural be men caves, or is it always one man per cave?"

"We're changing the name of the Man Cave," Reese informed us. "It attracts the worst kind of visitors. So many beer cans to dispose of, afterwards... and you don't want to know about the state they leave the bathroom in.

Last time, it was three guys on a stag weekend and they left a whole steak in the toilet."

"I have so many follow-up questions!" said Paisley. "But I don't think I want the answers."

"I'm thinking of upgrading that one to the Gentleman's Cave," said Bry. "Touch of class!"

"Yes, that will definitely help," Reese said dryly.

Bry, still winning the prize for least grumpy brother, answered questions while he rummaged in what turned out to be an entire cupboard full of homemade jam.

"You've seen the cottages, right? The signs are a bit bodgy, I had to do them last minute at the beginning of last summer when we first opened the cottages for hire, and we've never quite got around to fixing them. But they look aces inside. They were these old falling-down sheds when we took over the farm, we pretty much rebuilt them from scratch. Perfecting our reno skills. Anyway, there's the Love Shack — Annie and Guy Archer are staying there this week. Longterm married, kind of seem to hate each other. Then there's Harris, this old British birdwatching bloke? He's in the Man Cave."

"I have to see these cottages," said Paisley. "I hope the Love Shack has a water bed."

"It does not," said Reese, checking on his scones.

"Oh, and Pam was in the Belfry, last one up the hill," said Bry, looking a little sombre. "She wanted privacy for her writing or whatever. Wow. I wonder if she has any next of kin. What are we going to do with that typewriter?"

If Pam had headed out for an early morning walk in the direction of the creek, she wouldn't have had to pass any of the other cottages. How had her murderer known she was there? If I was a real detective, I'd probably have access to her phone and email, and I'd know if she had made arrangements ahead of time to meet a stranger. Or a fellow guest. Or one of her farmstay hosts.

Surely, if there was evidence on her phone or email that Pam had arranged an early walk with one of the farm guests or residents, the police would have already arrested them.

"Too much to hope it was the script for Vamp Pash 3 she was writing on that typewriter," Paisley said sadly. "Can't believe the real Prue Scythe was here in Tassie, right under our noses."

"You are too young to care about those movies," I informed her.

"They're vintage, Sam, you know I love vintage."

"Early 2000s is not vintage, stop saying words."

"I studied it in Grade 10! It's practically *historical*."

Bry was laughing at us. Even Reese looked amused despite his dour expression for most of this visit. "Are you two siblings?" Bry asked.

"It's getting that way," I said grumpily.

Paisley held up a miniature goat. "Don't get maaaaaaah-d," they bleated.

"Knock knock, only us," said a cheerful voice — male, deep voice, local accent — as he pushed open the flyscreen door. What kind of person says 'knock knock' instead of actually knocking? "Whoof, you really are baking in weather like this!"

It was nearly 4pm. The heat of the day had mostly died down with a cool-ish breeze coming in through the flyscreen. I wouldn't have my oven on in this weather, but given that my task was to sit here and eat scones, I wasn't going to complain too hard.

This must be Guy and Annie, from the Love Shack. She squeezed in behind him, already looking uncomfortable, though that could be the warmth of the kitchen. Guy had stopped in front of her, trapping her between the door and himself while he made his cheery greetings. Clearly someone who liked to be liked, and didn't worry about whether that extended to his wife.

"Went down to Hastings Caves today," Guy added, automatically filling in the part of the conversation where anyone had asked him what he'd been up to. "Hell of a drive, but lovely spot. Nice and cool, eh?"

Annie finally managed to squeeze out from behind her husband and came around the table to find a seat. "Hello," she said with a genuine enough smile. "New guests?"

They were in their fifties, I'd say — both well-padded and greying, though Annie had made an effort to look nice with a light floral shirt over light green crop pants, and a pretty pair of sandals. Her husband had it all hanging out in a stained t-shirt and shorts that didn't fit properly.

"Sam's helping me with the chair refurbishment project upstairs," said Reese abruptly, which was news to me but seemed to be a good cover story. "And this is Paisley."

"They/them," said Paisley helpfully, just as Reese opened the oven and pulled out the scones.

A wave of oppressive heat washed over the kitchen. Small price to pay for fresh scones.

"That's nice," said Annie. "One of our nieces is a

lesbian," she added to Paisley. I'd heard worse responses to gender-neutral pronouns.

"Awesome," said Paisley diplomatically.

"So many genders these days, someone should make some sort of dictionary to keep track of them," said Guy with a sort-of laugh that everyone tactfully ignored. "Oh look," he added as another man — presumably the other cottage guest, Harris, "Here's our twitcher. That's the Pommy word isn't it, twitcher?"

"It's *a* word," said Harris, his tone cool enough to dampen the room. He was — well, he did look extremely British. He was very pale, probably not much older than me, with steel grey hair. He was in the right age bracket for 'recently and reluctantly retired' which was the aesthetic he was giving off. His summer clothes included full trousers and a long-sleeved shirt, which was probably for the best when it came to avoiding sunburn (his ears had already copped it, I noticed) but not a good call for a warm kitchen on a Tasmanian summery afternoon.

"Birdwatching," Guy announced to the room as a whole, in case we had missed the memo. "Don't see the point of it myself. Like nature documentaries. All done by drones now, isn't it? Not like David Attenborough actually parachutes into the icecaps to talk to penguins."

"He is about a hundred and twelve years old," commented Paisley.

"How dare you," I said automatically, but Guy's penguin rant had already drifted into a 'drones are taking all our jobs' speech, and it was clear by now that everyone else in this kitchen had learned to tune out anything Guy said. His random interjections bounced from segue to segue, never providing pause for breathing or anyone else to contribute.

"Oh, lovely, jam," said Annie, a woman after my own heart.

"Blueberry for you," said Bry, giving her a warm grin as he set out a tray of jam jars on the table. "Hadn't forgotten it's your favourite. Plus the usual raspberry, strawberry, apricot and cardamom… oh wait, cream."

Reese, who had already tumbled the oven-hot scones into a wide ceramic dish and set it on the table while everyone (mostly Guy) was talking, now brought a bowl of whipped cream out of the fridge, ready to go.

"Is this from your goats?" asked Paisley. "I've never had goat whipped cream before."

"We don't do it often," Reese muttered. "Goat milk is lower in butterfat, so it takes forever to whip."

"There's a little goat milk yoghurt in the scones, that's the secret ingredient to make them so fluffy," put in Bry.

His brother cuffed him lightly. "What part of 'secret ingredient' do you not understand?"

"You do spoil us," Annie put in, already carving through her first crumbly scone with a tiny cake knife.

"All part of the Farmstay Cottage experience," said Bry, his smile starting to wear a little at the edges. I wondered if anyone else had noticed that.

"Apart from the murder!" said Guy, with a cheerful air that made it clear he liked to say 'shocking' things in public. It was amazing he hadn't found an excuse to call us all snowflakes already. "You know about all that?" he added in the general direction of me and Paisley. "The murder."

"Hard to miss," said Paisley. They were still sitting on the floor, a little way from the table, more interested in taking selfies with the baby goat on their lap than anything scone-related.

This was for the best, because I already had my mouthful of perfectly balanced scone, cream and raspberry jam. So good, but it stuck to the roof of my mouth. I wouldn't be asking the hard-hitting questions for a while.

"Poor you," Paisley added with fake sympathy. "Must have messed up the whole holiday vibe, what with one of you dropping dead all of a sudden."

"Not really," said Guy, dismissing the thought that anyone might have actual human feelings about the dead woman. "Bit of excitement, really. Didn't know her."

"Had a few conversations, didn't you?" Annie put in, with the first real edge I'd heard in her voice. Not quite the doormat I was imagining, after all. "Quite cozy sometimes, out there having a smoke together."

"Terrible habit," said Guy, piling cream on jam so generously on his scone, there was no way it would all stay on… oh and there he went, sandwiching the other half on top. "Never anywhere to do it. Banned from all the build-ings, can't even puff within a mile of a restaurant. Anyway, had to pick her brain, didn't I? She was a writer. I'm going to write a book," he informed the room. "Thought she might have a bit of useful advice. But she never seemed all that interested."

I finished my mouthful of *seriously the most delicious scone I have ever eaten*, in time to ask a question of my own. "What's your book about?"

Guy's eyes lit up, while Harris, Annie and Bry looked

instantly panicked, as if I had said the worst possible thing. Reese just looked like he wanted to hit me over the head with a baking tray.

"Well," said Guy, puffing up his chest importantly. "It's about this dry cleaner, mysterious chap, very good looking, who gets away with murder, right…"

Paisley almost snorted, but pulled it back just in time.

Twenty minutes later, the scones had been demolished, and I knew more about dry cleaning than I had ever wanted to know. Some of it was actually professionally relevant to me, or it should have been with my love of fabrics, but somehow Guy managed to squeeze anything of interest out of the topic, even when combined with the various horrific murders he apparently planned to put in his book.

I still didn't know if the dry cleaner was the hero or the villain, possibly both?

It was becoming very clear to me that Guy had no actual interest in writing. He seemed to think if he had a "good enough story" then "publishers would handle that sort of thing, assistants to type it up."

I was starting to suspect that Prue Scythe had murdered herself to get out of another conversation with Guy Archer. Who could blame her?

At one point, he muffled himself with a particularly large scone, and I could see the whole group around the table breathing out in a shared moment of relief.

"Did you spend much time with Pam?" Paisley asked

Harris the birdwatcher, getting in before I thought of a good angle.

Harris, who had eschewed both the fluffy white cream and the homemade jam in order to spread his scones with the thinnest layer of butter, spoke in a robust, earthy English accent that I (with my recent obsession with British murder shows) could confidently pick as one of the northern ones.

"She didn't talk to me much," said Harris, chewing with a closed, polite mouth in stark contract to Guy, who was attempting to neck his scone like he had another pair of teeth somewhere in his throat. "I appreciated that about her."

A man of few words.

"She had a lovely sense of style, Pam," said Annie quietly, as if she had taken all this time figuring out one nice thing she could say about the dead person. "Nice cardigans. And such interesting jewellery. Lovely scarves!" She suddenly looked horrified at herself and retreated into her barely-bitten scone.

Paisley and I glanced at each other.

"Our guest was strangled," Reese said shortly. He didn't say "with a scarf" but I could tell we were all suddenly thinking exactly that.

Bry got up quickly, taking the teapot with him to refresh the pot. Any excuse to turn away from us all, I thought.

"That detail wasn't in the news," said Paisley.

No, and Inspector Rosenthal hadn't mentioned it, either. So much for having a man on the inside. Clearly everyone here at the farm was aware — probably because

Reese had found the body and raised the alarm. Presumably they'd all had time to have a look at the corpse before the police took her away.

I'd made the matching scarf that went with the dress that the dead woman had worn on her final day.

Why, though? Why get up before 6am and put on a custom-made evening gown identical to an outfit you'd worn fifteen years earlier? Why bother with the matching *scarf*?

Clearly Prue Scythe hadn't vanished from that film festival and then magically appeared here on the farm this summer — there were a whole fifteen years to account for in between. Hell, I'd emailed back and forth with her last November, when she first got in touch about the dress. What had she been doing all that time in between?

Someone, maybe Prue Scythe herself, had wanted to make it look like no time had passed. I might almost believe it was a stagy suicide, designed to make everyone realise straight away who she was. But strangling yourself was... well, difficult at best. Especially out in the open. Surely it was impossible to kill yourself and dispose of the scarf without an accomplice.

"Were you surprised to find out who she was?" I prodded. Surely the farmstay guests must all know about the Prue Scythe reveal, though they still referred to her as Pam. "Any of you Vamp Pash fans back in the day?"

"Teenage crap," said Guy, at the exact same time that Annie said:

"Oh, I loved those films." She immediately blushed and looked mortified as her husband snickered into the last of the scones. "I wasn't a teenager, of course. But I thought they were, um. Fun. Romantic. I used to go to them with my girlfriends."

"You know," said Harris, gazing into the middle distance. "I don't think I've ever seen an Australian film. I didn't realise you made them out here."

See, this is why locals make fun of the English. That and something to do with cricket.

"I am making you a list of the best ones," said Paisley, unlocking their phone. "You have to at least see Priscilla. And Muriel!"

"There are some more recent than that," I said.

Paisley sighed. "It's like you don't even know me. *Vintage*, Sam." They stood up carefully, still holding the tiny goat, and took a few more selfies for good measure. "Harris, what's your number? I am sending you a list of Australian film homework."

Harris made a long-suffering face, but grudgingly swapped numbers with Paisley with the air of someone who had teenage grandkids at home, and knew better than to argue with them.

5

THE SCONE PARTY BROKE UP NOT LONG AFTER GUY Archer masticated his way through the final scone, leaving cream on his nose and, improbably, the tip of one ear. Bry offered another round of teas, but the guests didn't seem inclined to linger, making their excuses.

"I wish they'd just let us leave," burst out Annie, fretting as she headed for the door. "Not that — I mean it's been lovely… the cottages are so very comfortable, but not being able to leave the area feels so constraining. We have a business to get back to by the end of the week. I've never taken this long away, and it's all gone wrong."

"Try and enjoy your holiday," I told her. "I'm sure this will all be sorted out soon. At least they're not stopping you doing day trips. Hastings Caves and all that."

Annie paled beneath her freckles and turned on Guy immediately. "I told you we shouldn't have gone," she accused. "What if the police wanted to question us again?"

"What are we going to do, hang around on a stupid farm all week?" he muttered.

They headed off, still complaining at each other.

"Such a charming couple," said Harris, letting the sarcasm blend through. "Nice to meet you all," he added, in exactly the same tone of voice.

"I need to feed the goats," said Bry, as Harris marched out across the verandah.

"Oh, me!" said Paisley. "I want to help. And possibly, adopt all your goats."

Bry blinked. "You do realise she's eating your shirt, right?"

Paisley's floofy white shirt was definitely now missing a cuff, the edges hanging raggedly around their wrist. The little goat in their arms was chewing, smugly.

"She seemed to really want to eat it," said Paisley. "It won't make her sick, will it?"

"Bridie ate a gumboot last week, I think she'll be fine. You will have to stop cuddling her before we get to the paddock, or Mina and Spike will get unbearably jealous."

"*One of your goats is called Spike?*" Paisley squealed. "That one's officially my favourite. Sorry, Bridie, you're dead to me."

Bridie, still peaceably chewing Paisley's shirt cuff, seemed fine with that state of affairs.

They headed out in a clump of people and goats, leaving me and Reese alone in the kitchen with a table full of scone crumbs, and jam-smeared knives.

"Do you want to see some chairs?" he asked abruptly.

"Go on," I said. "Spoil me."

～

It was clear that the renovations hadn't quite made it to the second floor. The lovely polished wooden staircase trailed into bare, unpolished boards up above. There was peeling wallpaper, and some charming 70s combos of brown and orange that had certainly seen better days.

"We're going to have guest rooms up here eventually, if I can't talk Bry and Mum out of it," said Reese. "Need the funds to plumb in some en suites first, though."

We kept going up…

The top floor was all attic. Australian houses often neglect the attic — the older houses tend to spread out rather than up, and it's rare to find pointy roof space used for anything other than insulation. But whoever had designed this farmhouse originally was big on getting every square inch of space out of the building.

This attic was an enormous triangular space. Bare boards everywhere, and a wide window at either end, plus several sky-lights illuminating a mass collection of antique, pre-loved and in some cases slightly broken wooden chairs.

So many chairs. I had assumed he was kidding about the chairs. There had to be sixty or so of them, stacked in uneven towers. They'd clearly all been repainted recently, at around the same time, using the same off-white paint.

"Next stage of our evil empire of farmhouse capitalism," said Reese, in neutral tones. "We started with the goats and gourmet dairy production, then moved on to the B&B cottages. Team Wee Goat Farm won't be happy until we tick 'wedding venue' off our list."

"And then… profit?" I suggested. He seemed deeply

unenthusiastic about Team Wee Goat Farm, which was interesting.

"Ha," he said. "Someday."

"So, tell me about the chair refurbishment project that I am apparently helping with," I said. "I warn you, I've never sanded anything in my life. Or whittled."

I got half a grin off him this time. Talking about things other than murder was definitely helping him relax. "It's a fabric specific job. Your specialty?"

"I'm listening."

"When my Pop died, he left us the farm. Including roomfuls and roomfuls of all his old stuff — not going to say he was a hoarder, but one of the downstairs room was wall to wall newspapers and old tractor parts."

"Plus, he hoarded chairs?" I ventured.

"Not chairs. Suits." Reese nodded towards a couple of large stacks of boxes in the far corner of the attic, where the roof became the floor. "He was an op shop fiend. Collected all sorts. Surprisingly flashy taste, considering I never saw him wear a suit in his life. I think half of these are from like, ballroom competitions and that sort of thing."

That… was a bit exciting actually.

"Don't get your hopes up," he warned. "A lot of them weren't in great shape when we came across the collection. Burn marks, moths… obviously, Pop liked a bargain. A brightly coloured, shiny bargain."

This was sounding *even more* my sort of thing. "We could probably take some of those off your hands…"

"None of that!" Reese said, almost teasing. "We're not selling, we're *upcycling*."

Ah, the magic word. "I can hook you up with a gang of teens keen to turn vintage suits into handbags. If that's your bag."

"Nope. It's chairs all the way." He swung one out from the mass. "Bry saw this on a TV show, got all excited about the idea. You cut out a cushion pad from foam, fold the fabric around it, staple gun, those strips of upholstery studs to make things fancy. And bingo."

It was actually a really great chair. Freshly painted, with a padded seat made from a violent orange tweed. It looked both retro and modern, and just the sort of thing that would make a fun wedding feature if you had sixty to a hundred of them ready to roll out.

"That's brilliant," I told him.

"Yep. So brilliant it took me a week. But I've got the technique down now. Don't worry, I'm not going to ask you to wield the staple gun. What I need is someone with fabric expertise to help me weed out what's worth saving. Some of the clothes are in a rough state, and I have no idea how to clean wool or satin without wrecking the lot."

I waited, eyebrows raised a little.

Reese shrugged, and offered me a quarter of a smile this time. "Look. I know asking you here puts you in a weird position. It's a police investigation, they won't want civilians tromping around looking for clues. Bry gets these ideas in his head. If having you around asking a question or two makes him less likely to panic and throw himself at the police confessing every time he ever nicked a Freddo Frog from the local shop, that's a bonus."

"So you don't actually want to hire me as a detective?" I wasn't sure if I should be offended or relieved.

Reese threw his hands up in frustration. "I don't know! Bry won't tell me why he's so sure the police are going to try to pin this thing on him. Which is weird because usually he's the king of oversharing. He's not wrong that Inspector Murphy was — I don't know, she had some kind of bee in her bonnet about him. Like she was waiting for him to mess up. I don't see why she'd suspect him over me."

Interesting. "Would you prefer it if you were the one under suspicion?"

Reese looked annoyed. "No. Maybe. He's my little brother, you know? I'm supposed to look out for him."

Yeah, I knew. I felt the same way about Trace.

"And we read that interview with you last year," he went on.

Ugh, the interview. Paisley had convinced me to do it. We had so much press nosing around the boutique after the Dye Bath Murderer was arrested. And we had a new Fashion Detective business to promote...

It had meant talking about the worst time in my life, when I was arrested and put on trial for fraud. Even though I was eventually found innocent, there's nothing quite like being treated like a criminal for months on end to make you feel like you're losing your mind.

"You know what it's like to be accused of something you didn't do," Reese said in a low voice.

"I didn't think Bry had been accused of anything," I replied.

"Not yet."

He had to know more than he was saying. And, by the sounds of it, Bry knew more than he was saying to Reese.

They were both extremely mysterious. But I didn't get a bad vibe off either of them.

And we had a room full of chairs. Plus, a treasure trove of fabrics to upcycle.

While I was thinking it over, I took a few steps towards the nearest window. From here I had a really great view up the hill towards the cottages. I hadn't realised you could see them from the house — the slope of the hill meant from the verandah and kitchen door, you could only see the wood shed, the goat shed with its large fenced paddock, and a tiny corner of the Love Shack.

From up here, you could see all the way up the hill to the Belfry.

Earlier, when I asked myself the question of who might have seen Pam-Prue-Pam heading out on that early morning walk of hers… why yes, the two Carmichael brothers had to be considered.

Scones or no scones. Good vibe or no good vibe.

I wasn't going to find out anything if I wasn't here on the scene.

"I tell you what," I said slowly. "I'm working morning shifts only at the boutique this week. If you're happy to hire me for the next three days, I can come by in the afternoons to go through these hoarded fabrics of yours, and maybe upholster a chair or two. That will give me an excuse to be on site during the police investigation, and I'll see if I can be helpful."

"Fashion detective undercover?" Reese suggested.

"You'd be amazed what a woman will do to get her hands on a collection of second-hand suits."

~

"I see you managed to keep me out of it for the next three days," Paisley complained when we were back on the road, driving to Kingston. They were scheduled for the afternoon shifts at Fashionably Late for the next three days — and yes, I knew that when I made my suggestion.

"Like it or not," I said. "One of those five people might be a murderer, Pais. I'd prefer you to work on this one from a distance."

"I'm not a child," they grumped at me.

No, not technically. But from my advancing years, twenty years old wasn't too far off.

"If you're distracted by tiny goats, who's going to do all the background research on our suspects?" I urged. "Someone has to do the computer stuff."

Paisley rolled their eyes. "You don't need a specialist to Google things, Sam. Everyone can Google things!"

"I can't Google things while upholstering chairs."

"Not with that attitude!"

"I promise you more tiny goats in your future," I said. "Just… hopefully after the right person has been arrested for murder."

~

I was still thinking about Pamela West — Prue Scythe — Lady Prudence Sotheby much later. I was home in bed, staring at the ceiling and definitely not falling asleep, despite it being after midnight.

It was an odd thing, to change your name. I did it when I got married. I remember how it felt, to be Samantha Greenwood instead of Sam Sullivan. Great, at first. Like this was my chance to grow up into who I wanted to be. Samantha Greenwood was a wife, a successful business owner. Samantha Greenwood got shit done.

Later, it began to feel like a trap: Samantha Greenwood was the woman whose husband became more distant, who cheated on her, who ran off with her personal assistant and framed her for his own crimes. Samantha Greenwood was in the news, on trial. Putting Sam Sullivan back on again was like a comfortable, safe coat. Sam Sullivan felt like *me*.

I knew people who'd changed their names — to reinvent themselves, to match their true gender, to have a work self vs a home self. Actors, authors… *film directors*.

Surely no one took on a new name lightly. The ever-so-English Lady Prudence Sotheby knew what she was doing when she created Prue Scythe, the perfect name for an irreverent Aussie film director with a taste for vampire stories.

(Was she Vanity Fall too, the author of the original Vamp Pash novels?)

So many people, all dead in a single moment of scarf strangulation.

Warm milk never works for me as a bedtime drink. Why would warm milk make anyone sleepy? Blerk. I'd had some solid results with ruby grapefruit tea, which I was still in the process of testing. After tossing and turning for too long that night, I got up and headed to the kitchen, only to find there was a light still on. Not Trace, obviously — pretty much from the second she gave birth to Daisy she became instantly unable to stay awake past 10pm.

No, it was Inspector Rosenthal. Isaac.

He was still dressed for the day, more or less. He stayed over with Trace a couple of nights a week, usually when Daisy was with her dad in a vague nod towards "let's not progress things too fast," though Daisy was well aware he was a thing in Trace's life now, and was dedicated to convincing him that a nine-year-old future surgeon should be allowed casual visitation access to the police morgue.

Despite all those sleepovers, I'd never caught him wearing pyjamas, and had no idea where he was stashing the toothbrush that he must have somewhere in our bathroom.

Police officers. Such stealth.

Tonight, his jacket and tie were missing at least, so he was almost in casual mode — sitting at the kitchen table, staring at his laptop. He glanced up as I came in, not batting an eyelid at my shorty-shorts and vintage She-Ra t-shirt that Paisley convinced me I could pull off as daywear (spoilers: I could not).

"Working late?" I suggested.

"Something like that." He frowned and paused whatever he was watching on the laptop. "You were at the Farmstay Cottages today."

Ah, someone had blabbed. Whichever guest was

feeding info to the police was clearly still at it. "Consulting about upholstery fabric."

"Sam…"

"Don't ask questions you won't like the answer to," I added quickly.

Rosenthal rubbed his forehead, looking tired. "Was the scarf really three metres long? I don't know much about scarves, but that seems excessive."

"You've seen the footage from the Diabolique festival. It needed to loop a few times for the effect." I went to the electric kettle to start making my tea. "It was the crinkly edges that gave me the hardest time, but I was quite proud of the results. Have you found it yet?"

I could feel his hard stare boring into the back of my neck. "We have not. Asking for any reason in particular?"

I drummed my fingers on the counter, waiting for the water to boil. Not really wanting to turn around. "*Was* it the murder weapon? I know she was strangled."

"Sam…"

"I made that scarf!"

"Luckily for both of us, you're not currently a suspect."

Neither of us said anything for a while after that. The kettle boiled. I made my ruby grapefruit tea. Turned around finally, to inhale the steam.

Rosenthal looked so very tired.

When in doubt, change the subject.

"It's all right, you know," I told him. "If you stay over more often. I know Daisy's not the only reason you and Trace are slowing progress."

I was seeing a therapist now, a few times a month.

Working through my trust and anxiety issues from my arrest and trial, not to mention the Dye Bath Murderer. It wasn't a magic bullet, but I was feeling a lot less vulnerable.

Sometimes it felt like Isaac and Trace were so busy treading delicately around me and my issues, they couldn't focus on their actual relationship.

"I'm not a naturally fast mover, as it happens," Rosenthal said calmly. "Tracy's full steam ahead, and it's all I can do to keep up. But I have tried to be considerate… I never want to make you uncomfortable in your own home."

Sure, he arrested me one time. He was still ten times more decent than Trace's awful ex-husband Rich. Or my ex, come to that.

"I'm getting used to you," I told him. "I hardly even think of you as police any more."

"Oh, that's very comforting."

When in doubt, circle back to the original subject, and hope the other person gets dizzy. "Something's bothering you, isn't it? About this case?"

Rosenthal hesitated, then turned his laptop around to show me a freeze-frame of Prue Scythe, showing off her sarcastic self at Sydney reporters. The Diabolique festival marquee was clearly visible in the background — also red and black, so her dress looked amazing. The long red scarf was looped effortlessly around her neck several times.

She looked smart and feisty. She didn't look like a woman about to be kidnapped — or about to have a mental breakdown and run away — or about to be murdered.

Those were the three most common theories about what happened to her that night.

"The thing is," said Inspector Rosenthal in a heavy voice. "I don't think the woman in our morgue is Prue Scythe."

6

NOT PRUE SCYTHE. HOW COULD SHE NOT BE PRUE Scythe?

"But," I said, not sure I had heard him correctly. "But, DNA says that she *is*. You got the tests back early and everything."

"Tell me about it," Rosenthal said sourly.

"How can it not be her?"

"It is her," said Rosenthal. "But I don't think *she* is her, if that makes sense."

"I can categorically inform you that this does not make sense."

Rosenthal hesitated for a moment, then unlocked the tablet sitting on the table near his laptop, and pushed it in my direction. "I shouldn't be showing you these."

"And yet." I was looking at crime scene photos. Much less fun than film festival photos. But if I wanted to call myself a detective, I had to be prepared to suck it up and look at the occasional dead body from time to time.

Still not as bad as having to look at them in real life, so we had that going for us.

The woman who had called herself Pamela West, and whose DNA proclaimed her Lady Prudence Sotheby, had been in her 50s, give or take a decade. This woman was carrying more weight than the Gothed-up glam film director she had supposedly been fifteen years ago, but she was also dead which tended to make a person look simultaneously older and younger than they should. Her hair was dark, cut short but a long way from that highly styled black bob.

No makeup. Which was probably a crime scene thing, though of course it could be a 'went for a walk at 6am' thing or even a normal everyday Pam West thing. So far my detective skills were being supremely unhelpful.

Her neck was covered in mottled bruising, which I tried not to focus on. At the edges of some of the images I could see evidence of the frothy red fabric that was viscerally familiar to me. She was still clothed when they took these, then.

But the *face*. I looked at the face, then up at the paused image of Prue Scythe. "I mean, she sort of looks related to her. But people age oddly. It's been fifteen years. I couldn't be sure either way."

"Wait," said Rosenthal, and scrolled through a couple of images on the tablet. "That one. Look at her ear. Then look at Prue Scythe's ear."

I looked. And yes, I did sort of see his point. "Prue's wearing big earrings," I mused. "And... does the camera make earlobes look longer?"

"I could swear it's a different woman," Rosenthal insisted.

"But DNA!" I said again.

"I have no doubt that the dead woman on the farm is Lady Prudence Sotheby. Her brother's coming out from England shortly to identify the body, which should clinch it. Not that he's seen her since the 90s. I just don't think *this* is Lady Prudence." He stabbed the freeze frame of Prue Scythe in frustration.

I thought about it. "No one ever talked about Prue Scythe's birth name until after she disappeared, right? She never mentioned it in interviews or anything. It was leaked to the papers afterwards, though I don't remember now what evidence there actually was. Everyone accepted it as a fact. The family never denied it was her. But… I guess it was a mistake."

Rosenthal nodded. "Which leads to the big question: if Prue Scythe was not Lady Prudence, who was she? And where is she now?"

"Isn't it a massive coincidence if someone killed the real Lady Prudence fifteen years later, while she happened to be wearing a replica of Prue Scythe's most famous dress?" I added.

Rosenthal held up both hands in the world's biggest shrug. "You're the expert on this frock. Do you think someone could have put the dress on her after she was dead?"

"I'm amazed that an alive person got it on without like, three assistants," I said, looking idly through the rest of the crime scene photos to see if there was a better shot of the dress. "What kind of shoes was she wearing?"

"Sneakers."

"Sensible for an early morning bush walk."

"That's what made me think perhaps she wasn't wearing the dress when she left her cottage."

"Did you find any other clothes tucked under a bush?"

"No."

"Bit of a reach, Isaac."

"Fine," he grumbled. "You tell me why a woman would get up before dawn and go for a walk on her own, wearing an evening gown with sneakers."

"The sneakers part is obvious. Walking near a creek in heels would be stupid."

"And the gown part?"

"She was meeting someone she wanted to impress?" I mused. "But no. Dressing like a film star first thing in the morning is more likely to send a man running for the hills. It's too weird to be hot, you know?"

"If you say so."

"Was she wearing makeup? Her face is clean in these images."

"Hang on." He shuffled through them, found one. "Before they cleaned up the face."

Huh. Full face of slap. Even lipstick, though it was smudged. A dark red, the right fit for the dress. That had taken her some time. "She was wearing the dress on purpose if she matched her lipstick to it. Her phone was on site, was it?"

Rosenthal gave me a wary look. "We located it near where the body was found yesterday. Under several centimetres of silt in the river, which likely means no usable data coming off it."

I waved a hand, dismissing that as irrelevant. "So she was down at the creek with her phone. Glam dress, glam makeup, comfortable shoes. Early morning light. She must have been filming herself. Or taking selfies. To get the most of the dress."

He looked mystified "Why?"

"For whatever social media she has. Does she have social media?"

"Not that we have been able to find."

I rolled my eyes at him. "No one commissions a replica gown from a famous celebrity crime to wear at home while typing their novels. And even if they *do*, they put pics of it on Insta. Maybe Tiktok. I'm not 100% sure how Tiktok works, but if I was into it, and I had a killer dress, I would wear the dress while making Tiktoks." I shook my head. "What I don't understand is how she could have been so close to all those tiny goats and not think about adding at least one of them to her pics. Wasted opportunity."

"You realise this woman was older than either of us?" said Rosenthal. "You really think she was *that* into social media?"

"There are nannas on Tiktok! Anyway, she's supposed to be an author. They have to promote themselves some-how. Or maybe she was just sending pics to her friends." I shrugged. "Anyway. That's what makes sense to me."

"It's a better theory than someone strangling her and dressing her up afterwards," Rosenthal considered. "But *someone* wanted us to connect her to Prue Scythe, even if she is not Prue Scythe."

"Show me the dress again." I flipped through some

more images. "Shame I never got to see it on her while she was alive…" I made an undignified gargle noise.

"What?" Rosenthal leaned over to see what I was looking at.

I held up the tablet. This image showed a close up of the dead woman's mid-back, showing the dress. "Someone altered this. There's a whole extra *panel at the back.*"

"So it would have been easier to get on?" Rosenthal mused, then looked at my face. "You seem upset."

"Do you know how long we worked on that dress?" I howled. "Paisley was up until all hours for a fortnight. We offered free alterations if she'd only come in for a fitting, we *warned* her we couldn't guarantee a perfect fit without that. And instead she just — did it herself? The fabric doesn't even match well. It's two shades off the right red. We had spare fabric we could have *provided.*"

"Sam," Rosenthal said gravely, holding his hand out for the tablet. "Please stop giving yourself a motive for murder. I have enough to deal with."

"Customers are so ungrateful," I huffed, taking several angry swallows of my cup of tea.

"Try some of mine." After a moment, he gave me an amused sort of look. "So what else did you find out today?"

More gulping of tea. "Can't imagine what you mean."

"I know you spent the afternoon at Wee Goat Farm. Trace spilled the beans."

"Traitorous sister," I said. "It's almost like she likes you."

"I'm a lucky man," he said calmly. "Anything I should know?"

"Reese Carmichael is a very attractive man who bakes scones to die for," I informed him.

Rosenthal nodded, accepting this fact. "He probably did it, then."

"Ha ha. I'm going to be helping the Carmichaels out with some upholstery over the next few days." Best to not keep secrets from the in-house police presence. All above board.

"That seems like a perfectly good excuse to hang around a murder scene," Rosenthal replied. I was starting to learn that his version of sarcasm was saying things without any inflection at all.

"It's an upholstery *emergency*," I assured him.

"Well. That's all right then." He gave me an awkward, sort-of-sympathetic look. "You know this isn't my case, right? I'm not leading it. If police raid the farm again looking to make an arrest, I'm not likely to be there."

I looked at him in surprise. "But. Didn't you spend yesterday searching the place for the red scarf?"

"You're not supposed to know about that," he grumbled.

"It's kind of obvious. Everyone at the farm knows I made the murder weapon, and you're looking for it. Why aren't you in charge?"

"It's not my case," he said again. "Inspector Murphy was tied up most of yesterday talking to some very forthright English lawyers representing the Sotheby family. She asked me to co-ordinate the search on site with the uniforms, to look for the scarf and the phone. We were 50% successful."

"See, they do need you," I urged.

"I'll be helping out if they ask again, but otherwise —" He tapped the tablet. "Not my job."

"Oh." That was alarming. I had never met Inspector Murphy, and I'd been hanging on to the reassuring thought that if the police came back on site while I was nosing around, Rosenthal would be with them. Funny how quickly he went from being my worst nightmare to being the one police officer I trust.

"It should be fine," I said finally. "I mean, I'm not even slightly a suspect."

"I'm sure the upholstery consultancy could be managed after an arrest has been finalised," suggested Rosenthal. He was well aware of how anxious I got around the police. I still felt it around him sometimes — I couldn't help myself. But therapy was making a difference, and his presence in the house helped with that. Also him being so much better for Trace than her dirtbag ex-husband.

It didn't stop me being extremely anxious around all other police officers in the world.

"Everything will be fine," I said uneasily. "Upholstery must come first."

Morning shifts at Fashionably Late are my favourite. Living only a couple of short suburban blocks from work is the best of all possible commutes, even if I now walk the long way to follow where the river comes out at the beach, then along the beach strip.

The shorter way has some unpleasant memories I haven't yet managed to shake off.

This month's window display was Vintage Summer, all parasols, sun hats and retro swimsuits. We'd made a bunch of these up new, because the actual market for pre-loved bathers is unsurprisingly small.

Morgaine, our boss, even sifted through a stack of 70s women's magazines to find a pattern for a crochet bikini which she made using yarn from a jumper she'd unravelled the week before. She displayed the finished piece along with pieces of the printed pattern.

(There was a large sign attached saying Do Not Get Wet to warn potential buyers about the risks of knitted swimwear.)

We have three mannequins in regular use: Sheila, Kylie and Bruce. All retro, reclaimed and lovingly repainted. They're as much members of the Fashionably Late family as the staff.

"Morning, Morgaine!" I called as I came through the front.

"Morning, Sam." My boss is in her 40s, a solid woman with thick wavy hair she dyes dark red, and an uncanny ability to match items of clothing that really shouldn't go together.

Today she was in layers of cheesecloth and embroidery, topped off with a knitted vest covered in rosellas, and bright green sandals. Three fabric roses in the same colour as the vest were pinned into her hair.

"I hear you're branching out," Morgaine said to me as I walked through to the kitchenette, checking the jobs list on the white board. Laundry for me. Always a joy.

"What do you mean?" She'd been cool about Paisley

and I playing fashion detective up until now. Was she going to put a stop to it?

But no, she sounded amused more than anything. "Upholstery isn't for beginners, you know…"

I popped back into the shop. "What else are two grown men going to do with several bushels of fancy old suits?"

"I'd make handbags out of them, but each to their own." Morgaine gave me a stern look. "Paisley told me about the murder business. You stay safe."

"I'm barely investigating at all," I promised her. "A tiny snack of detecting, with a big dollop of fabric consultancy."

"I should think so! Good staff are hard to find. I don't want you ending up in a ditch somewhere. I hope you know about strip studs, don't let anyone tell you it's a good idea to bang in every pin individually."

Oh, and we were back to upholstery tricks. "Got it!"

Paisley called later in the morning, when I was putting freshly washed fabrics out on the line. The secret to selling second-hand — and adding value by upcycling — is that the clothes have to smell good. No musty or smoke-laden fabrics in this shop!

I'd have to share some of my tricks with Reese — or maybe upsell him to let Fashionably Late take on the fabric cleaning & restoration. We were equipped, after all, with multiple washers and washing lines. Like most Australian properties, they probably only had one measly Hills Hoist.

I had wireless earbuds in so I could talk and work at the same time. "What have you found out about our suspects?"

"We'll start with Pam West herself," said Paisley. "That's the easy one, because there's nothing. Literally nothing. She doesn't exist."

"Her social media presence is private?" Just because the police hadn't found it, didn't mean it didn't exist... unless it did mean that? In which case I was very confused about why she had been taking selfies. For dating apps, I suppose. Or maybe DIY author photos.

"She doesn't *have* a social media presence." Paisley sounded genuinely unsettled by this revelation. "Like, who doesn't at least have an old Facebook they never update? She's old enough for a Myspace, even. Or a Livejournal."

"Fake name, then." I thought about it. "They said she's a writer. So she doesn't write under the name Pam West. Maybe she's not published yet?"

"She doesn't do anything under the name Pam West. She doesn't exist, Sam."

"What name does she write under, I wonder?"

Not Vanity Fall. I might live under a social media rock of my own, but I'd definitely have heard something if the mysterious author of the Vamp Pash books made any kind of comeback.

"That is information that would be helpful to know," Paisley said thoughtfully. "Will Reese and Bry let you search her cabin? Maybe there are secret writer clues, like a notebook with her pen name written on it and underlined three times. An engraved plaque on her typewriter. That sort of thing."

"That will depend on the police," I said, shifting uncomfortably on my feet. Not good old 'I'm getting used to him' police like Inspector Rosenthal. Unknown, new-t0-me police. "Do you have anything else for me?"

"The suspects!" Paisley added gleefully. "Annie spends a lot of time on the internet. Pinterest, mostly, though she also spends a lot of time on Reddit advising women in relationship crisis that they should leave their husbands. So much time. Hours and hours. It's her major hobby."

"I can see it. I'd probably do that too, if I was married to Guy."

Paisley continued: "I'm not 100% on this one, but I did find a fanfic account Annie has sent a lot of likes to which is all about the vampire romance pairings. I even found an unfinished novel-length Vamp Pash coffee shop AU that I swear she wrote."

"Send me the link for that?" I said curiously.

"Already sent! First coffee shop AU I've ever read that knows what a flat white is. Oh, and *Guy*, he's all about writing comments to articles in their local paper online. He is the definition of why you don't read the comments."

"Not that I'm not impressed with your levels of internet stalking, but what do you know about them in real life?"

"The internet is real life, Sam," Paisley said sternly. "But I accept your feedback, moving on. Their dry-cleaning business has a solid four-point-two-five star rating. Annie is clearly the front-of-house person, because all the nice comments from customers are about her.

There's a few 'the dry cleaner kept going on about this book he wants to write, what a bore' comments too. Enough to make it very clear that this Guy and Annie are real dry cleaners, not impostors."

"I wasn't thinking they were imposters…" I said slowly.

"Aha. That's what you need me for, Sam. You're so trusting. Ask me about Harris McBritishface, the bird-watcher. Go on, ask me."

I rolled my eyes at the wet laundry. "Hey, Paisley, what have you found out about Harris the birdwatcher?"

"Wait for it," said Paisley. "This is where is gets interesting. He signed the guestbook Harris Taylor, but his real name is Marmaduke Harris."

"His name is not Marmaduke," I said, caught in awe at the very thought of it.

"Okay, I lied, but Marmaduke is more fun to say than Mark. Most of his appearances online only give the initial and I'd already fallen in love with calling him Marmaduke when I found his real name."

"How did you know he used a fake name in the first place?" There was a lot of that going around.

"I did a reverse image search, and he came up as a… Get this. Actual legit private detective. The Harris Agency in Manchester, England."

"Why would a private detective put his image on a website? Wait, did you say reverse image search?"

"Yeah, you know. When you want to find the source of a picture, so you run it backwards through Google?"

"That's a thing?"

"OMG Sam, how have you been tracking vintage buttons across the world without knowing this basic trick? Anyway, I did that. His photo is on the website because he's like the big boss of the agency. It's not one guy with a bottle of whiskey in a desk drawer. It's this whole corporate investigation agency."

"He's not retired, then? Just happened to pick Tasmania for his birdwatching holiday?"

"Nah, because get this. The Harris Agency is big enough to have a Board, and one of the board members is the Honourable St John Sotheby. That's a real name, by the way."

"Relative of Lady Prudence?"

"Either her youngest brother, her father or her great-uncle. They're so posh they keep re-using the same name. Probably all share the same tweed jumper, too."

"This is very good detective work, Pais."

"I know," they said smugly. "Bry thought one of the guests had been telling tales to the police…"

"Our Brit detective is the most likely option," I concluded. "Do you think he came out here to track down Lady Prudence?"

"I mean," said Paisley. "He found her. Clearly. Massive coincidence and major shade on his detecting skills if it wasn't deliberate."

It really was.

"Wait," I said. "How did you even get a photo of Harris in the first place, to search for him online?"

Paisley snickered. "You didn't think I was really just taking goat selfies that whole time you lot were stuffing yourself with scones, did you?"

I had, actually. "You literally have put eight goat selfies on your Insta today."

"That's because I am a multitasker, Sam. Admit it. You're lucky to have me on your side."

Of that, I had no doubt.

7

ONCE MY FASHIONABLY LATE SHIFT WAS DONE, I borrowed my sister Trace's car to head back down in the direction of Grove, and Wee Goat Farm.

I really needed my own vehicle, especially with all these detective jaunts. Morgaine was nice about lending me her car, but I only felt right about asking if it was for official Fashionably Late business — Paisley and I should be able to stand on our own two feet with Fashion Detective work.

And Trace, being an estate agent, needed her car most of the time. I was lucky she was volunteering at the school this afternoon, which was within walking distance of home.

My finances were still not in great shape after the great destruction of my life a couple of years back. My old assets had been frozen and eventually sold off because of my husband's crimes. I'd been in a credit card black hole when Trace saved me with a cheap living option.

Working part time at a boutique was exactly the low-stress job I needed, but it wasn't doing much to put a dent in my debts, or allow me to build up savings. A car of my own wasn't quite on the horizon.

I knew Trace wouldn't kick me out any time soon, but... she had Isaac now. Things were getting more serious, even if he was still only at the stay-over-a-few-nights phase. The house — belonging to Trace's ex's dead Aunt Harriet — wasn't something I had any claim over. I didn't have to worry about her moving in a new boyfriend quite yet, but... at some point, I was going to become the weird lodger who lived with her sister's family.

Fashion detective was an interesting pastime, and I was not going to say no to three afternoons of upholstery-and-asking-questions paid at an hourly rate.

But sometime soon I was probably going to have to start making some decisions about what my future would look like.

Bandit and Chilli welcomed me enthusiastically as I drove up to Wee Goat Farm. I could hear the rhythmic sound of someone chopping wood like his life depended on it, and when I got out of the car I saw Bry with his back to me, taking some frustrations out on the woodpile.

Reese was in the kitchen, clearing away the remains what looked like an epic lunch.

"Sorry, there's not much left," he said, heaving an empty pie dish into the sink and filling it with water to soak. "I can do you a sandwich?"

"You don't have to feed me," I told him. "Do you...

have to feed everyone else? I thought you didn't do meals."

He pulled a face. "New round of police today. They made it very clear that all guests were to stay on the premises for now. No more tourism jaunts for Guy and Annie. They were not happy about it. Bry thought putting on a lunch for the happy couple would help keep them sweet."

"It did not?" I ventured.

"It did not. They were yelling at each other when they headed back to the cabin. Which is honestly better than them yelling at me." He looked exhausted. "At least Harris had the decency to accept a lunch tray in his cabin. I don't think I can deal with three meals a day of guest-wrangling. At this point I'd be willing to drop everything and plumb kitchenettes in so they could cook for themselves. But they'd probably complain about that too, and I'd be done for tampering with a crime scene." He took a few deep breaths. "Sorry. You don't need this. I don't need this."

"I mean, while we're on the subject," I said. "Any chance I could get a look around the Belfry? Or have the police taped off the cottage?"

"They've taken it apart and put it back together again, but no police tape," Reese mused. "They said it was okay for me to clean it. So I guess... want to help me clean it?"

"You're very good at getting people to help you with your work," I observed, as he whisked a cleaning bucket out of a nearby cupboard and we set out again into the warm afternoon.

"Ah, that's my mum's influence," he said. "She had this superpower of doing everything all at once in a way

that made you feel guilty for not helping. And somehow…
there were the rubber gloves, there was the mop, and away
you went. If we learned anything from her, it was how to
get things done."

"Is she involved in the farm?" I asked, since I hadn't
met her yet.

"Here and there," Reese said vaguely as we made our
way up the hill. I didn't press him on it.

Despite the quirky sign suggesting that the Belfry was
the home of bats and possibly the Count from Sesame
Street, the cottage was the same wooden chalet design as
the other two. Inside, the main feature was polished wood
— the floor, the walls, etc. The furnishings were in warm
cream with touches of dramatic red — throw cushions, a
dark rug.

Not a grain of dust anywhere, I noticed as Reese set his
bucket down on the kitchenette counter. The whole place
had a hotel room neutrality about it. Few signs that it was
inhabited. "Did the police take Pam's belongings?"

I couldn't think of her as Prue, let alone Lady
Prudence. So many different people to keep straight.

"I don't think so," said Reese, looking around. "They
might have taken a few things, they've been back and forth
for days. I already emptied the fridge. But there's some
books and things over there, clothes in the bedroom, bathroom stuff. Unless they've been in again since yesterday."

The books were what I think of as airport novels — the
kind with the author's name much bigger than the title, and
lots of silver bling. Romantic thrillers, both written by P.S.
North. There was a pencil with the books, but no sign of a
notebook.

In the bedroom, I really did feel like I was the nosiest creep in Nosy Creeptown. Pam hadn't been tidy — her clothes were tossed over chairs, the chest of drawers. There was even a bra on the polished floor.

The bedclothes had been pulled straight but not made properly — I guess the police didn't provide a full turn-down service.

Her vintage typewriter, and a half typed manuscript, were set up on a small desk by the window. I cast an eye over the pages: a paranormal mystery, by the looks of it, about a witch called Cassidy, her talking owl, and her werewolf spy love interest.

The suitcase, jumbled with clothes, lay open. I didn't want to touch it. Really, I shouldn't touch anything — the last thing I should do was leave traces of me all over this cabin.

There were more books on the bedside table. I took a photo of the spines with my phone, in case it could be useful.

When I got back to the kitchen, Reese was cleaning the countertop, almost absently, like it was what he did the minute nothing else had to be done. "Find anything interesting?"

"Apparently, I feel very guilty visiting other people's bedrooms when I haven't been invited."

He shrugged. "You get over that fast, running a B&B. You wouldn't believe some of the things people leave behind, like it never occurs to them a real person will see their trash. Seen the bathroom? Bry considers it his best work."

I went back to have a look — only when I was inside

the bathroom did I see that the back of the door was covered in small replicas of old vampire films. Dracula for the most part. It's amazing how many Dracula films there have been, all in all. The posters were pretty cool — a little larger than postcard size, clearly printed and varnished for this purpose.

They weren't all vintage. I spotted Twilight and a few other more recent films — including (and I was refusing to think about how old it was, but *less than 20 years is not vintage, Paisley*) the original Vamp Pash, right in the middle.

"Must have been odd for her, walking in and seeing that one," I remarked.

Or maybe not. After all, Rosenthal didn't think this Pam was Prue Scythe. I wasn't going to tell anyone that detail — I knew he probably shouldn't have told me.

"Mum was a big Vamp Pash fan back in the day," said Reese. "Bit of a wild child. She did management for rock bands, never around much when I was little. But she loved vampire stuff. That's how we ended up with goats named after Lestat, Jean-Claude, Count Duckula… oh, and Caaarmilla, of course."

"Ha! Of course."

The only goat name I remembered was Bridie — Bride of Dracula, perhaps?

"I remember finding her Anne Rice collection when I was ten," Reese went on. "And reading like… way more Anne Rice novels than a ten year old should. Scarred me for life."

"Did you watch the movies when they came out?" I asked, still looking at that poster. "Vamp Pash, I mean."

"Nah, I was too young. They wouldn't have let me in the cinema. I caught them on VHS later, though."

I blinked a few times. For some reason I'd assumed he and Bry were… well. My age. They were running a whole farm, after all.

Vamp Pash may have included vampires and kissing but somehow it managed to skirt under the M rating to PG 13+ here in Australia. I'd just been old enough to see the first one at the movies, as the first one was released shortly after my December birthday.

"How old were you when the first one came out?" I asked, trying to be subtle about it.

I heard him laugh, on the other side of the door. "Like, eight."

"*Are you twenty five years old?*"

I hadn't been thinking about him romantically. Not at all. At least, I didn't think I had. But the fact that I was panicking about a six year age difference suggested that maybe I had in fact been thinking that.

Good thing there was all this murder to stop me throwing myself at a handsome farmer who was a tiny child when the Vamp Pash movies came out. Apparently that was my boundary.

"Twenty six," he said, still sounding good humoured about it.

"That's young to be running a whole farm like this."

"Bry's twenty four."

"You're both babies!"

Bry was closer to Paisley's age than mine. And apparently had been flirting with our fifty-plus murder victim. I guess age wasn't something other people got hung up about.

I'd married a man only two years older than me, and it ended in disaster. Catastrophic disaster. Age wasn't a factor. Trace married someone exactly her age and it was — well, not worse than how mine ended, except that at least my ex had the good manners to commit a crime and leave the country so I didn't have to see his stupid face and be polite to him all the time like with Richard the Worst.

Trace was maybe fifteen years younger than Isaac Rosenthal, and I'd never seen her happier. You never can tell.

Wow, I was rambling now. At least I'd managed to keep it all inside my head.

Reese popped his distractingly good looking face around the bathroom door. "Got everything you need?"

"Not sure yet," I said, following him out to the living room. "When did Pam book her stay?"

"I'd have to check the records," he said, frowning. "Well in advance, though. November, maybe? Annie and Guy booked like, six months ago. They had a voucher."

"And Harris?"

"He was last minute. Called the day before he arrived, last week. We'd had a cancellation in the Man Cave, or we wouldn't have had room for him. Once we get the upper floor of the main farmhouse renovated, we'll have more space, so Bry says, but after this week I'm not keen to have guests under the same roof…"

"What's on the back of the bathroom door of the Man Cave?" I asked suddenly, curious.

"Action movies. You know. Mad Max. Gladiator. The

ones about cars that are both angry and speedy."

"And the Love Shack? Rom coms," I guessed, speaking in unison with him for the last part.

"From His Girl Friday to When Harry Met Sally."

"Have you noticed Harris talking to the guests, asking them questions about themselves? Did he take any particular interest in Pam?"

"No. You've met him. He's anti-people. Only thing he seems less interested in than people is, well. Birdwatching."

Huh. That was odd. A real life private detective somehow managed to do his job without asking a bunch of nosy questions and raising people's suspicions. Was he magic? Pretending to be interested in people is the only way I ever find out anything. Speaking of which…

"If your mum was so involved with the farm, why isn't she any more?" I asked.

Reese gave me a cagy look. "Why do you ask?"

"I am extremely interested in people. Especially fellow Vamp Pash fans."

"Her health isn't great," he said shortly. "She was trying to do too much when she was here, and we encouraged her to take a break from it all. She still handles our online bookings. Answers emails. Office stuff. She hasn't spent much time up here on the property this summer."

He was radiating discomfort with the topic.

"So she never met Pam?" I asked.

That question surprised him. "No reason she would. What's your fascination with my mum, anyway? She has nothing to do with any of this."

I could tell I had irritated him. Most people would back

off at that point. I used to work in the wedding industry —
I know the sign of someone who's at the end of their rope.
But my job isn't to soothe the trouble brows of brides,
grooms and their families any more… it's to wash and
repair upcycled clothes and sometimes, to solve mysteries.

You don't solve mysteries by soothing brows. Irritating
people gets the job done much faster. Which means
fighting my natural tendency to placate.

"I'm curious," I told him.

"It's none of your business."

"Well, now I'm *really* curious."

He gave me the most impatient of impatient looks.

I spread my hands wide. "You literally hired me to ask
nosy questions. I don't know what I need to know until I
know it."

Reese picked up his cleaning bucket with the
maximum grumpiness possible for that basic task. "I hired
you to upholster chairs and make sure my brother didn't
get arrested," he snapped.

I gave him my 'the customer is always right' smile.
Most people find it unsettling, me included. "Let's upholster some chairs, then."

As we headed out of the Belfry, I glanced back at those
books stacked on the side table. Something about the pen-
name was gnawing at me. P.S. North. Our Pam had called
herself Pam West. In another lifetime she had been known
as Prudence Sotheby. Patterns are almost as useful for
detectives as they are for dressmakers. "Can I take those
books?"

Reese was already out the door, striding ahead of me.
"Knock yourself out."

8

AS WE HEADED BACK TO THE FARMHOUSE, WE HAD TO PASS both the other cottages. I saw curtains twitch in both cases. The inmates were restless.

Bry was done with wood chopping. He headed past us with a loop of wire over his shoulder and a pair of pliers in his hand. "Fence to mend," he informed his brother. "Hi, Sam."

"Hi, Bry."

"He throws himself into work when he's stressed," Reese said, as we headed into the kitchen.

"Admit it," I said. "You both throw yourself into work when you're relaxed too, right? Neither of you ever seem to stop."

His mouth twitched. "That's farming for you."

"I wouldn't go back to being a small business owner if you paid me," I said with conviction. "Get it?"

Reese huffed. "Come on. We have chairs to work on. At least I can be doing something productive while you ask your nosy questions."

"Here's a fun one for you," I said as we headed up the stairs. "Why are you so sure Bry is likely to be arrested? From where I'm standing, your brother is the one least likely to have done it. You're the one who found the body, right? He would have had to get past you, plus the three cottage guests, there and back, without being noticed. All before it was even light."

Reese gave me a long, measured look. "So, who's the one most likely to have done it? It sounds like you're saying it's me."

Oops. No putting that goat back into the barn. "You'd have to be very confident," I said after a moment's thought. "To believe you could bluff the police about having innocently found the body and *then* hire a detective to investigate the crime yourself."

He raised both eyebrows. "So you don't think it's me?"

If I've learned one thing since accidentally becoming a fashion detective, it's to never actually tell someone to their face that you think they're a murderer. "I'm not ruling anything out. If you wanted to look as innocent as possible, you probably could have found a private detective who doesn't specialise in fashion." It was possible I had been spending too much time with Paisley. Usually those were the thoughts I kept inside my head.

Reese looked at me like he couldn't believe I was real. "So, chairs?" he said finally.

"Chairs," I agreed.

I still wanted to know why he was so sure the police were likely to arrest his brother, but I wasn't going to push him too hard. Most days, it's all I can do to avoid people pouring out all their deep family secrets.

Give him time.

~

There's nothing like a good old repetitive task to give you thinking time. I used to appreciate those times when someone — always me — had to fill a hundred bonbonierre bags, or tie sixty peach ribbons to sixty place cards.

I did some of my best project planning that way. These days it's mostly the Fashionably Late laundry that gives me those calm thinky moments.

Today, it was more fabric sorting than upholstery. Reese and Bry's grandfather had hoarded enough glamorous dance suits to start a rental business — if they were in better shape. Unfortunately, he hadn't been quite as dedicated to storing them properly as he had to acquiring them — some of the suits were damp, most were musty, and the moths had definitely had a party or two.

The smell was bad enough once all the wardrobes were open that Reese immediately opened all the windows, which meant a warm and sticky afternoon handling satin and sequins.

"Guy and Annie are dry cleaners," I observed at one point, as I started sorting armfuls of old jackets into piles — what could be used straight away, what needed to be washed or at least aired out properly, and what definitely needed more help than could be done in three days. "Did you think of asking them for advice?"

"I thought about it," said Reese. "But then I thought about being stuck up here with Guy talking about how he's going to write a book someday, and I figured I was less likely to throw myself out the window if I asked you."

With smooth talking like that, a girl might feel light-headed. No, wait, that was the elderly velvet fumes.

"What are you planning to use the chairs for?" I asked as I sorted.

"I told you. Bry and Mum's epic wedding business plan. Because why run two businesses when you could run three…"

"I mean, indoors or outdoors. Upholstered seats in these fabrics are a bad idea in Tasmanian weather. If there's even a chance they'll get wet, you want to be able to remove the cushions in a hurry."

Reese looked demoralised. "Hadn't thought of that. We have an old barn down on the lower paddock we were going to turn into a banquet space, but for ceremonies it's likely to be hired marquees or open air." He groaned and leaned back against a few chests of sparkly trousers. "I thought we could have them ready for the refreshments tent at the race on the weekend. But now I wonder if we should ditch the whole plan."

"I've been meaning to ask about that. Is miniature goat racing an approved sport?"

"Nah, it's just a bit of fun. They mostly run in circles and bump into each other. It's, like, slightly above slug racing."

"Why do it?"

"Because it's stupid and fun, and somehow Bry's moments of genius always come down to stupid and fun. We did it one year as a joke and half the locals came for a big paddock party. Now everyone expects us to do it. At least if we're selling tea and cakes we might not make a loss this year."

"You have a lot on your plate," I remarked.

"All the more reason we'd like to put this police business well and truly in the rear view mirror." Reese looked around the attic. "Okay. Where do we start? Or do I throw up my hands and tell Bry we should set fire to the lot of it?"

"How many chairs do you need for the refreshment tent?" I asked.

"Fifteen or twenty. It's not a huge tent, and most people move around with their food. It's just to provide shade for those who want to sit down with a cuppa, the older folk, mums with bubs, that sort of thing."

"That's doable if we figure out which fabrics we want to use today," I said decisively. "I can take some with me to wash and air out, bring them back tomorrow."

"Okay," Reese said, smiling like a small weight at least had been taken off his shoulders. "Let's do it."

While I sorted fabrics, a job I could practically do it in my sleep thanks to all the estate sales I'd visited with my boss, I thought about what I'd learned so far about the mysterious death of Pam West, who was also Lady Prudence Sotheby, and possibly not legendary Vamp Pash director Prue Scythe.

I thought about Harris the private detective, and how he had to have known Pam was staying here. If he knew her brother from her Lady Prudence days, it couldn't be a

coincidence he ran into her while on a birdwatching holiday. He had to have come here on purpose, either to find
her or to meet her.

Ugh, it was no fun doing this without my crew. I
needed Trace and Paisley and a big whiteboard to bounce
ideas off. Later. Tonight, maybe.

My thoughts kept returning to that dress Paisley made.
That perfect, made-to-order red gown, based on all that
iconic footage of Prue Scythe's last public appearance.

I delivered the dress two days before Pam died. And
someone had altered it — cut it up and inserted a panel in
the back, with fabric that wasn't even a decent match.

Obviously it had been a bit too tight — enough that she
needed to go up half a size or so.

Who had done the alteration? Why had Pam allowed
such a bodgy mixup instead of contacting us and asking us
to do it professionally? She obviously wasn't short of cash
— We'd charged her $1200 for the original reproduction,
and then we showed the invoice to Morgaine and she made
us charge an extra 25% on top because we were selling
ourselves short.

Pam hadn't blinked at the charge. Why cheap out at the
last minute, wrecking an expensive dress? What was so
urgent that she had to take the scissors to it?

Only, she hadn't taken the scissors to it, had she? Not
personally. There was no sign of any dressmaking tools in
her cabin. No scraps of fabric, no fabric shears, not even a
spool of thread.

"How often do you clean the cottages while the guests
are there?" I asked Reese.

He shrugged. "Depends on their preference. They have

the option of weekly housekeeping, daily, or every two days. We don't let them stay longer without at least getting in there once a week to empty the bins and wipe down the bathrooms."

"Smart. When did you last clean the Belfry, before Pam died?"

"Maybe three or four days before. Then straight after the first police search, to empty out the fridge and such."

"Did you find any fabric?"

"Sequins or satin?" He held up a ragged purple jacket that amazingly had both, as well as velvet lapels. It looked like it had escaped from Strictly Ballroom, but Strictly Ballroom had put up a fight.

"Ha. I mean, red fabric. Like the dress. Scraps of fabric, thread…" Oh, I was an idiot. "Is there even a sewing machine on the property?"

Reese looked at me oddly. "I mean, yeah. Mum's old one. We haven't used it in years. Bry tried to alter curtains about six months ago and made a right tit of himself."

"Can I see it?"

"Sure." Reese wasn't paying attention to me. He stood by the windows, looking across the yard. "What's Harris doing poking around the goat shed? He should know better than that."

"I mean, he's English," I said dubiously. "Aren't they all — you know, fields and cottages?"

"Only in All Creatures Great and Small. Oy!" he called out through the open window, then pulled back. "Bry's got him."

"Bry's got something," I said, joining him at the window.

The usually sunshine, easy-going Bry looked in a real state. His voice was raised, though from here I couldn't hear what he was shouting. He gave Harris a shove in his chest, and Harris moved quickly, getting him in a professional-looking headlock. Not bad for someone hovering at retirement age.

"Hey!" Reese yelled, and dropped his armful of sparkly jackets on the floor, heading for the stairs.

I scrambled after him.

What on earth had Harris said, to make Bry react like that? Hopefully Reese would reach them in time to prevent the fight getting nasty.

As I followed Reese down the stairs to the kitchen, the dogs started barking wildly. By the time we made it to the door, I heard another sound that made my heart freeze.

A short warning siren — BLIP BLIP. Two police cars pulled up on the gravel outside the farm house, blue lights rotating overhead.

9

POLICE MAKE ME ANXIOUS. I SUPPOSE THAT'S TRUE OF A lot of people — I know many who say that the sight of a police car or uniform makes them instantly paranoid that they might have done something wrong. That frisson of guilt, mixed in with the knowledge that chances are at some point they *have* done something wrong. Even the most law abiding members of society have walked off with something they meant to pay for, gone a few k's over the speed limit, or performed a little light jaywalking when no one was looking

After my court case, when I was proved innocent of my husband's fraud, after the whole nightmare of being arrested and living in fear of a prison sentence, after losing my house and my car and the business I'd built up over most of my adult life… after all that, I discovered that people really like to confess their own run-ins or near-misses with the police.

"Everyone feels a little anxious around a cop car," One

former colleague said, like they were discussing a minor inconvenience.

It wasn't like that for me. For months after my arrest, the sight of a police officer — even a perfectly nice one, like round-faced Sgt Arthur Torrance who is attempting the world's slowest courtship of my boss Morgaine — filled me with a freezing dread. I couldn't walk, couldn't talk. Couldn't think straight. Sometimes I couldn't quite breathe normally.

It's getting better. Having my sister date Inspector Isaac Rosenthal — the very officer who arrested me, and to his credit now feels a bit bad about it — has served as a form of exposure therapy. And yes, I invested in real therapy too, which has been incredibly helpful. I still wasn't comfortable with the idea of meeting police on duty who were not Isaac or Arthur.

In that moment, standing on the threshold of the Wee Goat Farm kitchen, I discovered that yes actually, I was still bloody terrified of the police.

Some detective, huh?

Reese was over by the nearest goat shed, having just pulled his brother roughly away from Harris. Several small goats were pushing their faces through the paddock fence, clearly wanting to get in on the fight.

The three men stood staring at the police car. Harris straightened his shirt with the air of a man who wished he was wearing a tie. Bry radiated innocence, while Reese looked like he wanted to strangle them both.

A stern looking woman, tall with solid shoulders in a suit and tie, got out of the first car, along with Sergeant Deng. He was of Sudanese descent, dark-skinned and almost as long-legged as his current partner. He usually worked with Inspector Rosenthal, who was half a head shorter than him.

I didn't recognise any of the uniformed officers from the other squad car, but it was the kind that has a locked hold at the back for arresting prisoners. Mesh windows. All extremely intimidating.

I was busy trying to breathe in and out like a normal person, so my usual observation skills were not at their best.

"Inspector Murphy," the tall woman said, introducing herself in a curt voice. "Which of you is Bryson Carmichael?"

Bry awkwardly raised a hand. "Can I ask what this is about?" he asked, acting like someone who hadn't spent the last two days panicking about being arrested.

"We managed to dry out the victim's phone," said Inspector Murphy. "It's amazing how robust they are, these days. We'd very much like to discuss that phone's contents with you, down at the station."

"Hang on," said Reese abruptly. "Is he under arrest?"

"Shut up, Reese," Bry hissed at him. "It's fine."

Inspector Murphy gave Reese a very cool look. "That all depends," she said. "On whether he is willing to come down to the station and have an informal chat with us."

The word 'chat' was far too friendly to have come out of her mouth.

"It's fine," Bry said again. "I'll come."

"I'm coming with you," Reese insisted.

"No one else is required at this time," said Inspector Murphy. "Just Bryson Carmichael."

Reese looked gutted.

Bry, of course, was pretending everything was fine. He got into the back of the car with Deng and Murphy, and they circled around to the driveway.

The other uniformed officers stood by their car and said nothing.

"You're not going with your mates?" Reese demanded roughly.

"Protective detail," said one. "We've been asked to stay on the property. Keep an eye on things."

Reese shook his head and stormed towards the house — towards me.

Harris caught him up on the verandah, touching his arm. "Reese. Do you or your family have a lawyer?"

Reese stared blankly at him. "What?"

"A lawyer," Harris repeated. "Do you have one?"

"We have one who handles estate business, contracts." Reese stared at the older man, not quite comprehending.

"Call them," Harris said. "Now. Get him to arrange a criminal lawyer to join your brother at the station. Go to Legal Aid if you have to. But get it done in the next ten minutes."

Reese looked panicked. "Is that necessary?"

"Only an idiot would talk to the police if they didn't have to, without a lawyer present," said Harris, his Manchester accent broadening as he spoke. "Your brother doesn't seem all that smart."

Reese nodded, and hurried into the house, calling the

dogs to follow him. I stepped out of the way to let him through.

Harris met my curious gaze. "Something to say, Samantha Sullivan?"

Reese had never introduced me to the guests with my full name. But of course...

"You're a private detective," I said, keeping my voice steady. I did not like the police being so near, leaning against their car and chatting like they had every right to be here.

"So are you, I believe," said Harris.

"The Sotheby family sent you here?"

"Someone was claiming to be their long-lost relative. It seemed appropriate to check it out."

"And was she? Their long-lost relative."

"I'm sure you read the news. DNA doesn't lie."

"Where had she been all this time?"

"The middle of nowhere, apparently." He dismissed the farm around us with a small wave.

"Rude."

Harris laughed. "People give more away when they're annoyed."

Well, now I just wanted to grill him for detective hints. No! No getting distracted. He was still a suspect.

"What was your fight with Bry about?" I asked curiously.

Harris didn't seem like he had anything in particular to hide. "He took exception to my proximity to the goats. Livestock can be so sensitive."

"And why were you sniffing around the goats?"

"I object to the word sniffing, though they do have a certain fragrance, don't they?"

I raised my eyebrows at him, waiting for him to answer the question.

Harris shrugged. "I noticed during the previous police searches that they didn't pay much attention to the goat shed. Since we still have a murder weapon to find, I wanted to nose around. In fact, I'm going to do that right now. Since young Mr Carmichael is busy trying to keep the other young Mr Carmichael out of jail."

He turned and headed towards the paddock. I probably should have called out to Reese or tried to stop Harris, but at this point how could him finding the missing scarf make anything worse?

Also, I was pretty sure the goats could take him.

I wasn't alone on the verandah. Annie Archer was quietly tucked into one of the battered old armchairs, watching the remaining police car nervously. I knew how she felt.

"Sorry," I said, heading over to her. "I didn't see you there. Are you okay?"

"I've never seen anyone arrested before," she said in a hoarse whisper. "Do they really think Bry killed that woman? He's such a lovely boy."

"He's just going to assist them with their enquiries," I said, in what was hopefully a soothing voice. "He doesn't seem the violent type, does he?"

Annie shook her head. "But you never know, do you? With murders. It's always the one that people least expect."

Ah yes, that classic trope which owes so much to Agatha Christie, Midsomer Murders, and the like.

"In real life, the most obvious murderer is usually the one who did it," I told her.

"Oh. Really?"

"Boring but true. Real murderers aren't that smart."

"In that case," Annie said surprisingly. "I probably did it. I didn't like Pam at all."

"I don't like lots of people," I said with a laugh. "I don't feel driven to murder them. Unless there's something more you want to confess?"

"Oh, no. Except the bit about not liking her. You feel so guilty, don't you? If someone dies and you can't even feel a little bit sorry about it. I felt like that when Guy's mother dropped dead. She'd been so horrible to me, it was so hard to get through the funeral without laughing."

Now, this was interesting. "What didn't you like about Pam?" I pressed.

Annie looked hunted, like she hadn't meant to say so much. "She was one of those women, you know?" she prevaricated.

I tried to look interested and encouraging. 'One of those women' could mean so many different things. "What kind of woman?"

Annie took a deep breath. I could see her deciding to trust me. Me and my open face struck again. "*You* know. She'd be friendly enough to other women in a distant sort of way — unless there was a man around, and then she'd be all about him. Playing up to him, flirting, giving him all that dazzling attention. It was like a performance, but she cared about some audience members more than others."

"She flirted with your husband?"

Annie laughed a little. "Oh, I knew she wouldn't be interested in Guy in a million years. But she acted like she might be. All their little talks, smoking together after hours. In-jokes, that breathy laugh of hers. It's almost worse, you know? She didn't want him. But she wanted me to know she *could* have him. She was the same with Bry — not really interested, but playing the game."

"She was a lot older than Bry." Old enough to be his mum, if my maths meant anything.

"Oh, that didn't matter to her. I suppose it was all about the reeling in. She wasn't looking to catch anyone."

"You say she flirted with Bry. Not Reese?" Both brothers were attractive. What did it say about me that I was drawn to the one who seemed to have more cares on his shoulders?

"Reese didn't like her," Annie said immediately. "And women like Pam, they want to be liked, don't they? She knew that Reese saw through her, I think. She was always approaching Bry alone, taking opportunities when Reese was elsewhere. Asking little favours, commenting on how strong he was. That sort of thing."

This was interesting. Reese had been very careful around how he talked about Pam. I'd never got the impression he didn't like her.

"Did she sound British?" I asked suddenly. "It must be weird to find out she wasn't Pam after all, but Lady Prudence. All very Downton Abbey."

Annie gave the matter some thought. "No. She was — very stagey. Posh Australian, you know? Maybe she was laying the accent on a bit thick. I thought she was from

Adelaide or something. Darwin. But she must have been here for ages. Decades."

Everyone thought Prue Scythe was Australian, too.

"You've been following the news about her?"

"I mean, what else is there to do?" said Annie. "Especially now we can't leave the property. Guy's furious about that. He had so many plans, a big list of things to do on holiday. And now he's stuck here with me." She gave a tragic little smile.

I fought the urge to offer to Google divorce lawyers on her behalf. If Pais was right about Annie's online activities, she was way ahead of me on that one.

"Did Pam go out much? Join you on any sightseeing activities?"

"She wasn't invited," Annie said firmly.

"On her own, then?"

"I don't think so. She mostly stayed in her cabin and wrote her book, when she wasn't prowling around the farm making eyes at men. Bit of a waste of a holiday, all that typing. You know we haven't had a real holiday in five years, me and Guy. I was really looking forward to this."

"So Pam didn't go anywhere off the property?"

Annie thought about it. "Into Huonville, I think. To the library once or twice — and I saw her at a cafe on the main road once, sitting in the window with her notebook." Her mouth turned a little mean. "I suppose she wanted everyone to *know* she was a writer. I'd never heard of her."

Huonville. It was the closest town. Big enough to have a supermarket — but did it have anyone who made cheap clothing repairs? I'd have to check that out.

(Though honestly, why would they have to be cheap?

Our own shop was half an hour away. We'd have done the alterations for free if she'd only been willing to come in for a fitting. Or, you know. Asked. She couldn't be that short of money if she could spend several weeks at a rented holiday cottage, not to mention lugging a vintage typewriter on a plane.)

"She didn't write under her own name," I said absently. At some point I was going to have to find the time to Google the name of PS North to see if my guess was correct. Paisley was wrong — the way things were going I definitely did have to outsource looking things up on the internet.

"Oh," said Annie, looking almost disappointed. "I suppose that makes sense."

"What about Harris?" I asked, peeking over in the direction of the goat sheds. "You didn't mention him. Did Pam make eyes at him? Flirt at all?"

"Not with him," Annie said immediately. "It was rather awkward. She pretended he wasn't there. Blanked him entirely. I assumed he must have said something offensive when I wasn't around. But we were all here when he arrived. No one really had time to offend anyone."

I'd bet that wasn't true when it came to Guy Archer, but I took her point.

"Did you get the impression Pam and Harris knew each other already, then?"

Annie's face lit up, like she had some killer gossip she had been busting to share. "She went to his cabin once, late at night. I was so surprised, because she'd always ignored him. Maybe that was how she treated the men she really wanted to sleep with."

"You think they slept together?"

"I was out on the verandah listening to my podcast, because Guy was watching that show I hated, the one with all the girls climbing things and falling off things. It was after ten PM. She knocked on the cabin door, never said a word and Harris just let her in. I assumed she stayed late, or stayed over, because I never heard her leave."

"Which night was this?"

"Not the night before they found her. The police would have been more interested if it was that night. The one before that."

So, the same day I had delivered the dress.

"You told the police?"

"That Inspector Murphy," said Annie. "She interviewed us. Kept asking if we'd seen anything odd the night before. I told her all about it, even though it didn't happen *that* night, because it seemed relevant. I told them about the camera, too."

"Camera?"

"Video camera. Pam was holding it when she went to Harris' cabin. One of those big ones, with a strap. Handheld but very, you know. Professional looking. She always took it with her when she went on one of her walks. I suppose she was off being artistic. Anyway searched all over the property and I'm certain they never found it."

So the police had been hunting for more than Pam's phone and the missing scarf when they ransacked the place. Good to know. I bet they didn't think to search for a sewing machine.

Amateurs.

~

When I made it inside the kitchen, Reese was sitting at the big table looking defeated. Chilli and Bandit nosed around his feet, matching his mood. Good dogs.

"You got on to a lawyer?" I asked.

"Yeah. Much good it will do. Knowing Bry he'll have told them every bad thing he's done since kindergarten already."

"I mean, that shouldn't take too long, right?"

"He'd be done before he got to the station," Reese said glumly.

"But you do think there's something," I pressed. "On that phone. Not because of what the Inspector said — but you already knew there was something that would look bad. That's why you brought me in — why you were so sure he'd be arrested. I can't help unless you tell me everything."

Honestly, I wasn't sure I could help at all. Not now the police had Bry in their sights.

If he was innocent, I would do everything I could to help him.

But from the look on Reese's face, I wasn't so sure any more that Bry was innocent.

10

WHEN YOU WANT PEOPLE TO TELL YOU SECRETS, MAKE
them a cuppa.

Even in their own kitchen, with their electricity, their
teabags and their crockery, somehow it makes them feel
comforted and looked after. Making a cup of tea (or coffee,
or in extreme situations, hot chocolate with marshmallows)
for another human being automatically makes them trust
you slightly more.

True fact.

If there are biscuits involved, all the better. Even if the
other person literally baked the biscuits, the act of you
putting one in front of them… well, you get the idea. It's
manipulative, but it does the job.

I was pretty sure Reese had baked these biscuits. They
were shortbreads, good and crumbly, with a cherry-sized
blob of jam baked into the top, just like my Nan used to
make.

I put two in front of him, on a saucer decorated with
chickens, and a large mug of strong tea.

"So," I said encouragingly. "What's on Bry's phone?"

Reese gave me a wary look.

I pointed at myself. "Once again, you *hired* me to ask nosy questions. And I'm much better at that than stapling cushions to chairs." To be fair, I still hadn't stapled a cushion to a chair. No, actually, that proved my point.

"It's not what you think," was the first thing he said.

A promising start. "Don't worry about what you think I think. Just out with it. Rip it off like a band-aid."

Reese poked absently at the mug of tea, and ate a biscuit. "Right. So Pam had been smooching up to Bry. He's always a bit of a flirt, but there was something, I don't know. Targeted about her. She wanted something from him."

"He's a grown man."

"And I left them alone!" Reese said defensively. "Didn't hassle either of them about it, despite the extremely sketchy age difference. No judgement from me. But things got weird."

"Weird how?"

He frowned. "I got the sense Pam was avoiding me. Always coming up with excuses for the two of them to go off alone. Something went wrong with her hire car early on, and she never replaced it. Bry was always giving her a lift into Huonville, or wherever she wanted to go."

"Nice of him."

"Yeah, he's a pushover. Anyway, there was that, but then they kept disappearing together."

"Disappearing? Where did they go?"

"I don't know. It had to be somewhere on the property. They'd just — not be around. For hours."

I raised my eyebrows. "I mean. Given the evidence. That's really not all that mysterious?"

It wasn't hard to figure out what two people with a mutual attraction might be up to, with a convenient cottage nearby.

Reese rolled his eyes at me. "Yeah yeah. Only, Bry swore blind they weren't shagging. And there was no reason for him to lie about it. Plus he's the world's worst liar. Turns bright red, even over stupid stuff. I didn't get the vibe that either of them planned to take the flirting any further. It wasn't that."

Huh. "So what were they doing?"

Reese gave the world's biggest shrug. "I don't know! He still won't tell me. Whatever it is, though, there's a record of it on her phone. Bry is usually Mr Chilled Out, but he was going out of his skin during the early police searches. And when that other Inspector — Rosenthal? Found it in the creek, but waterlogged. Bry was relieved when he thought the phone was wrecked. Like someone had taken the weight of the world off his shoulders."

A lot of things could be found on a phone. "Is there anywhere on the property that someone might be able to hide things? Some bolt-hole the police might still not have found?" It seemed unlikely considering how many full property searches had been conducted by now. But Harris thought there might be something worth finding in the goat shed. "Maybe somewhere only you and Bry know about."

An invisible tree-house. Nuclear fall-out shelter. Floor safe under the compost heap?

Reese looked troubled. "Why would that matter? They got into the phone already."

"Annie told me that Pam had a camera. Like, a high end video camera. Harris knew about it. I don't think the police have it yet. There was also a scarf that went with the dress. Given that Pam was strangled, and how keen the police are to find it, I think it was what the killer used." I'd got that directly from Rosenthal, but I didn't mind Reese thinking it was one of my brilliant detective discoveries. "And that's not all." There were those the leftover threads and scraps from her dress alteration, assuming they hadn't been binned directly. I couldn't get them out of my head. "Is there anywhere in Huonville that does dress alterations? Sewing?"

Reese pushed the plate of biscuits towards me. Oh, no, he had discovered my secret interrogation technique. "Why do you ask?"

I sighed. I really shouldn't let this bug me. "Because I delivered Pam's dress less than two days before she died in it — and it had been altered to fit her. So someone with sewing skills put a dodgy new panel in the back. But I haven't found any evidence that it was done here."

"That's why you asked about mum's sewing machine. Come on. I'll show you." He brought the mug of tea with him, which I took as a personal victory.

The sewing machine was in a room on the first floor, bundled in with a whole pile of boxes and other crafting bits and pieces. My favourite kind of room: messy and full of treasures.

"This used to be Mum's room, but she stays downstairs

these days, when she visits for the weekend," said Reese. "I don't think anyone's used the machine since Bry's mad attempt at curtains. It's definitely the only one we have."

I pulled the lid off the machine and had a bit of a poke around. The last threads used were teal and orange. "Those are from the curtains?"

"The colour combination was the least catastrophic choice he made that day," Reese said solemnly.

No red threads. So unless someone altering a dress at high speed decided to conceal every trace of what they were doing by replacing the original spools afterwards — for no reason I could think of — this machine had not been used on Pam's dress.

"I don't think she took it anywhere," Reese said from the door, still nursing his mug of tea. "Inspector Murphy asked all of us, that first day, whether Pam had left the property recently. Bry remembered taking her into Huonville earlier in the week. But I don't reckon she left the place after she got the dress. Two days before, you said?"

"Less than. And she didn't ask Bry to take a parcel anywhere for her?"

"He never mentioned it. And he would have done. The police asked a lot of questions. It would have come up, right?"

"You tell me." I glanced at my watch. "You still have an hour with me on the clock. Want to sort more fabrics?"

He laughed, clearly about as invested in upholstery as I was. "Nah, not really. But it's something to do. Take my mind off what's happening with Bry. How long do you reckon it will be?"

"That depends a lot on how good his lawyer is. And whether they decide to arrest him."

I myself had once spent an awful, confusing, grim night in the custody of the police, before I even realised the extent to which my husband had screwed me over.

"Fabrics," I said firmly, and led the way.

Reese and his mug of tea followed me.

"You're not actually thinking about chairs right now, are you?" Reese asked a little while later.

I had stopped pretending to sort satin linings, and was just digging into box after box. It must be obvious that I was looking for something.

"It's that extra panel in the back of Pam's dress," I confessed. "The fabric had to come from somewhere. It wasn't an exact match by a long shot. But still. How did she get hold of that lengths of red fabric? And what did she do with the leftovers and thread? Why is that something that anyone would even bother to hide?"

Not to mention: how did Pam alter the dress in less than two days without access to a sewing machine? I'd seen the crime scene photos, no way those seams were hand-sewn.

"You're very frock-driven," Reese said thoughtfully.

"It's my specific area of interest." When I learn something, I learn hard. I learn everything. A few years ago, it never would have occurred to me I'd have the skills to dye a replica evening gown, or to solve mysteries. "Did Pam ever take selfies around the farm?"

"I guess so. With the goats. Most people do."

"But did she?"

He thought about it. "No, actually. Annie and Guy did. Harris definitely didn't — I'm not sure I've even seen his phone."

"Maybe he doesn't have international roaming." He'd given Paisley his number, though. I'd have to ask them if he ever replied to that string of film recs.

"He got that look on his face when he saw the Archers doing it," Reese added. "Like he wanted to say something mean but was holding back. I don't think I ever saw Pam take a selfie. Does it matter?"

Maybe it did. It was possible I was overthinking it. I do that.

If she wasn't a selfie-taker, why was she all glammed up by the creek first thing in the morning? Formalwear for Facetiming? Getting in a crafty Zoom call before breakfast? Maybe she was a shy selfie-taker, only willing to do it when she was absolutely sure no one else was nearby.

"The trouble with your grandfather's taste," I said aloud. "Is you're going to end up with a lot of sparkly chairs."

"He didn't just buy suits that belonged in a ballroom dancing competition," said Reese, back to his usual setting of 'grouchy'. "There's definitely a crate of old brown wool suits here somewhere."

"Those will be even *better* if they get rained on!" If there was elderly wool in this attic, surely I'd have smelled it already.

"Maybe we should just paint the chairs," he sighed.

"You mention this now?" I hauled over an old travelling trunk which looked about a hundred years old, like something out of a World War II movie where children get sent away from London to be safe from the bombs. I pawed through the shirts inside, bringing up some lighter shades. Most people wouldn't think to upholster with shirt fabric — it just wasn't a as hardwearing as the stuff from jackets and trousers, but maybe with the right interfacing… "See, this is more like it. Lavender and lilac stripes, perfect for a summer wedding!"

Red flashed between my fingers as I brought up a handful of fabric. Familiar, silky microfibre, good enough to pass for silk in a good light.

"Hey," said Reese, his voice cracking. "Is that — the missing red fabric you were talking about?"

"No," I said softly, turning around. The length of it poured from my fingers and looped back into the box. I kept pulling. I knew this fabric. I knew those stitches. "This is the missing scarf."

In other words, the missing murder weapon.

"Oh, hell," said Reese, looking pale.

My sentiments exactly.

11

"IT'S FINE," I SAID ON THE PHONE TO ISAAC ROSENTHAL
for like, the third time. "Of course it's fine."

I was sitting on the stairs, near the ground floor of the
farmhouse. Obviously I had to report this discovery to the
police. That's what you do when you find a murder
weapon. Reese had been all for crossing the gravel out
front and telling the uniforms, but the thought of that had
me quietly freaking out. I didn't know them. I didn't know
how they'd react, or how they'd treat me.

To Reese's credit, when he saw whatever he saw on
my face (I was trying to be cool about this but it clearly
wasn't working!), he asked me what I wanted to do.

Apparently, I wanted to call the one police officer I had
recently started to trust, and put the whole matter in his
hands.

But Inspector Rosenthal couldn't come out to the property today. This was not his case, and he was tied up with
something else at work. Couldn't get here in time. He
sounded almost as upset about it as I was.

(He had guilt issues, thanks to my anxiety around the police… and I kept trying to make him feel better about it, and around and around we went in our mutual spiral. Thank goodness Trace would have the ability to soothe us both with delicious tiny food, and repair any awkwardness until next time.)

In the end, Rosenthal tipped off Inspector Murphy to come back to the property and take custody of the new evidence, with the reassuringly familiar figure of Sergeant Deng following behind her. It would do. It was fine. Everything was fine.

(I guess if she was here, she wasn't at the station in Hobart giving Bry a hard time… right? She couldn't police in two places at once.)

Chilli and Bandit barked protectively from the veranda as the inspector walked, straight-backed, into the kitchen.

Wow, she was tall.

"Show me," she ordered Reese, who led her upstairs to the attic. I probably should have gone with them, but I was feeling a bit wobbly. I made tea, instead. When in doubt.

"Cheers," said Deng when I pushed a mug in his direction. He looked like he had been dying for a cuppa all day.

"What's it like working for her?" I asked. "Compared to the Inspector." *Our* Inspector, that was. Deng knew what I meant.

"Different," he said fervently. "She's mile a minute, this one. It's all smoothies in the car, no proper lunch breaks. Kale smoothies," he added, sounding mildly distressed.

"You should talk to your union about that," I joked.

"Yeah." Deng gave me a bit of a grin.

Look at me, making conversation! That what I call progress.

It all got a bit less cozy when Inspector Murphy returned to the kitchen. She saw Sergeant Deng, sitting at the table with his legs stretched out in front of him, and gave him such a judgemental look that he leaped to his feet, spilling a little tea as he went.

Her main attention was on me, however. She wasn't rude, but direct. I felt the weight of her eyes on me. "And you are?" she demanded.

"Samantha Sullivan." Surely she must have known that already. This felt like being called in front of the principal for wearing my skirt too short.

No, worse than that. After my arrest, and all the way through to my trial, I spent a lot of time around police officers. Some were respectful, or cautious around me — either because I was an emotional wreck who kept bursting into tears, or because they saw me as the kind of entitled white woman most likely to make a complaint if there was any hint of poor treatment. I was never quite sure.

During that time, I saw a lot of flat, emotionless faces. Some of the worst officers, the ones who made me feel small and scared and completely vulnerable, were women.

Inspector Murphy had that same icy look about her as some of those officers. Under her piercing gaze, I couldn't seem to find any of the confidence or poise I'd been building since I got my life back.

What I wouldn't give for Diana Wave's *Confidence* jacket about now.

Inspector Murphy didn't ask anything else, so I kept going. Babbling a bit. Damn it. I know that technique. I use that technique myself. Unsettle people, ask questions, wait for them to tell you everything.

"I'm a friend of the family. Helping out with chair fabrics."

Was this lying? Should I tell her outright that I was here to snoop around on behalf of my clients, the Carmichaels? I definitely shouldn't tell her that. Unless Reese already told her, and she was waiting for me to confirm it.

I glanced at Reese, hoping for some kind of clue.

"Sam's been a big help," he said, coming to my rescue. "Like I said upstairs. My grandfather left us a hoarding mess. And we need those chairs in time for the Wee Goat Race."

"The race," I agreed, relieved. I still wasn't 100% sure what a goat race was for, but as long as no one asked me to explain it, we should be golden.

Inspector Murphy turned back to me. "And you're the same Samantha Sullivan who made the dress that the victim was wearing when she was found."

Found, she said, not killed. Was she working on the theory that someone had killed Pam and then dressed her up to the nines? I was pretty sure no one who had ever tried to wiggle into a side-zip evening gown would believe that theory. Maybe Inspector Murphy was more into pantsuits.

"No," I said quickly. "I mean, not exactly. Paisley

made it, a colleague of mine. We worked together. I dyed the fabric and helped out with some of the materials… and I made the scarf."

I could almost see her eyes glazing over when I started talking about the dress, but she zeroed back in on me when I mentioned the scarf. "How did you know the scarf was in that particular trunk?" she accused. It was an accusation, no doubt about it.

"I didn't!" I protested. "We'd been going through the fabrics all afternoon." Well, with a few breaks for sleuthing and cups of tea and Reese's brother being detained. "I opened half a dozen boxes and trunks. We were sorting through the lot."

Inspector Murphy's gaze flicked to Reese. "Did your brother have access to the attic, over the last few days?"

"You know he did," he said, sounding tired. "His room is on the first floor, same as mine. We're both in and out of the house all the time."

"Bry wouldn't have hidden the scarf there," I blurted.

They both looked at me.

"He wouldn't," I pressed on, feeling less terrified of Inspector Judgyface now someone else was her target. "It would have been stupid. He knew I was coming today to work on the upholstery project, right?" I looked to Reese to check. "Surely he would have known anything hidden in all your grandfather's old clothes would be found. If he was the one trying to hide something, he wouldn't put it there."

Of course, Bry could have hidden the scarf before Reese volunteered me for upholstery duty. But in that case, surely he would have nipped up to grab it back before I arrived. Unless he was arrested before he got the chance…

"Did your brother know about this project?" Inspector Murphy asked Reese.

"Yes. We've been talking about it for months. And Bry was here yesterday when I said Sam was going to help with it."

Of course, Bry also knew that Reese suggested the whole upholstery project as an excuse to get me on the property. Still, he must have guessed we'd at least make a stab at going through all the old clothes. Unless it was a double bluff? I was so glad I wasn't saying any of these thoughts aloud. I was here to help the brothers, not help them get arrested more efficiently.

(Assuming of course that they were innocent — and yes, I was assuming that. I probably shouldn't, especially after what happened last time.)

"Did anyone else hear your little announcement?" Inspector Murphy sneered.

"All the cottage guests," Reese informed her. "I don't think any of them but Bry knew what I meant by upholstery project, though."

"And if they did," I mused. "Bry had more opportunity than the rest of them to move the scarf before I found it. If he put it there in the first place."

"Funnily enough," said Inspector Murphy dryly. "We don't discount theories that rely on murderers making stupid decisions. They're not all diabolical masterminds. Some of them can barely read or write."

"Which trunk was it in?" Sergeant Deng asked.

We all looked at him.

He shrugged a shoulder. "We searched the attic on Day 1. Didn't we, Inspector?"

"Clearly not thoroughly enough," she snapped.

Or someone moved the scarf to the trunk after the first police search. I opened my mouth to say as much, then saw Reese wincing. No, it really was better to *not* say all my theories out loud.

Inspector Murphy gave me another of those piercing looks of hers, like she knew what I had been thinking. "Fancy yourself a detective, do you, Ms Sullivan?"

I smiled weakly. "Fashion detective only. With a special interest in rare buttons."

"So when you said you'd get my car back by six…" Trace called out teasingly from the living room as I let myself into our little house by the back door.

"I know, I'm sorry!" I said. It was after seven. Something else to feel bad about. "There was unexpected murder related business. And the drive back from the Huon is always longer than I think it's going to be."

"I was going to go to the supermarket for dinner!"

"I can go out again now if you have a list," I offered guiltily.

"So it's entirely your fault that I heated up a tray of bacon and mushroom canapés and started watching Vamp Pash instead," she announced.

Okay, now I was feeling less guilty. "Which one?"

"The good one."

"They're both good!"

I spotted some leftover canapés on top of the stove and made myself a plate, along with some salad and strawberries from the fridge. (Berry season in Tasmania is the best!)

When I entered the cozy living room (decor by the late Great Aunt Harriet, so everything is covered in quilts, hand-knits and/or tassels) I found Trace immersed in the last act of the first Vamp Pash movie, with puppy Demi curled up asleep in her lap. Fernando had just been revealed as a surprise villain, and was chowing down on the fragile neck of doomed Ruthie, which meant he was about three minutes away from being staked from behind with a fence post.

Yes, I've seen this film many, many times.

"Weird to think that the director is dead," Trace murmured, eyes on the screen. "But I suppose a lot of film directors are dead really, if you think about it."

"Comes to us all," I agreed. But I knew what she meant. The Prue Scythe mystery had been so huge when we were teens. Like Elvis, but for baby goths and book nerds. You'd hear about sightings of her in little towns all over Australia.

Huh. I guess some of those might have been true after all.

Prue Scythe might be dead now (unless she wasn't) but that meant she'd been alive all this time (but maybe not). Ugh, this was doing my head in.

"How did you go with your chairs?" Trace asked.

"One of them got arrested."

"Oh, shame."

Inspector Murphy had dropped that bombshell on

Reese at the last minute, as she left the farm with the scarf in an evidence bag. She told him they were keeping Bry overnight, with a bail hearing tomorrow. It sounded like the arrest had happened before the scarf was discovered, but it certainly hadn't helped his case.

When I left, Reese was on the phone to his mother and their family lawyer, trying to figure out what was happening.

Trace and I watched in silence now as Carmilla ran on to the screen, armed with a fence post still trailing barbed wire. She staked Fernando through the heart, turning him into a shower of dirt. She then sobbed over the dead body of Ruthie for about fifteen seconds, before Ruthie opened her eyes and tried to bite her neck.

There went the fence post, two for one.

"Carmilla was the best," said Trace happily. "You don't see her in things any more, do you?"

"She was in Play School."

"That was years ago. That was before *Daisy*, Sam."

Huh. It was a while since I'd checked in on the careers of my favourite actors. "Didn't she go to Hollywood? She was like, the second assassin in that movie about lady assassins. But that was years ago too."

"I think she became a personal trainer or something. Quit acting."

"Awww."

"Nah," said Trace. "People always act like it's a huge tragedy when show biz people go and live normal lives instead of showbizzing it up forever. But I always think — wow, now they don't have to paint on three layers of eyelashes every day. Must be so relaxing to just live an ordinary life."

"Trace. I'm pretty sure you're wearing three layers of eyelashes right now."

"I *choose* to do that. I don't *have* to because there are paparazzi hovering around the corner ready to tell the world I forgot to put a bra on before going on a coffee run."

"Mmm," I said in a vaguely agreeable tone.

Was that what Prue Scythe had done? Run away to live a normal life somewhere? Escaping the limelight by typing novels on vintage typewriters, and hiding in goat-themed bed and breakfast retreats?

Until, of course, she wasn't alive any more.

12

My day started early, getting Daisy ready for school. That way, Trace got a sleep in to make up for me keeping her car too long the day before. No worries there — Daisy is a great kid, as long as she's not hassling me about my potential cholesterol intake, or insisting we have extra vegetables with our meals.

Yeah, no, that's not really something parents (or aunts) are supposed to complain about, is it?

Our future doctor, nine years old, is currently obsessed with the health benefits of green smoothies, which was fine now she and I had both mastered the art of remembering to put the lid on the blender.

While Daisy was chopping pineapple and kale (kale! Apparently Dais and Inspector Murphy would get on like a house on fire) for our breakfast, then measuring in exact spoonfuls of plain Greek yoghurt, I finally did a bit of online research about P.S. North, whose books I had borrowed (stolen? Let's say reclaimed) from Pam's farm-stay cottage.

She was prolific, that was for sure. There were ten novels by P.S. North, all romantic thrillers from the same publisher, with giant silver letters on the front, thick doorstoppers with taglines like "You'll laugh your socks off" and "Who was Yvonne kissing when the plane crashed into a jungle?" and "Scorching action, sizzling sex scenes!"

There was no author photo. P.S. North's author website was glossy and vague as to the real person behind the pen-name, but it did link to her other pen-names. P.S. North, it turned out, also wrote sassy historical mysteries as Primrose Waters, and spicy urban fantasy novels as Persephone Severn. She'd been rolling out at least two books a year for the last decade, with Primrose Waters' back catalogue — featuring a glamorous lady sleuth in Hollywood's 1950s — going back nearly twenty five years.

I stopped myself before ordering a bunch of them, reminding myself that reading a pile of novels was not necessary research for solving a murder, and anyway they likely wouldn't arrive in time to make a difference.

Then I ordered the first of the Primrose Waters books anyway, because they looked excellent, and I'd probably want something relaxing to read after I solved the murder.

"Is that you?" Trace called to me from the bathroom when I returned from walking Daisy to school. "Isaac called."

"It's sweet how your boyfriend still uses landlines," I said, stopping outside the door. "Clearly he time travelled here from 1935."

"Don't knock it, the man has manners. He thanks everyone when we go out."

"As opposed to your ex who liked to make waitstaff cry."

"That only happened once, and I had already decided to divorce him!"

"What did Isaac want, anyway?" I checked my phone. "Never mind, he texted me."

"See?" said Trace. "He can twenty-first century if he wants to."

"It must be so sad for him that no one sends telegrams any more." I read the text. "I'm meeting him in ten minutes apparently, usual place. He'd better be bringing coffee."

"Some women might be put out by their sister and boyfriend having a special meeting place," Trace said in a sing-song voice.

"It's literally across the road, you are more than welcome to join us and the ducks."

"No, thanks, I want to preserve the mystique of how long it takes me to look amazing in the mornings."

"Hate to break it to you, but I think he knows you don't sleep with a full face of makeup…"

"Tell that to my three layers of eyelashes."

One of the best things about moving to Aunt Harriet's little weatherboard house in Kingston Beach, apart from the next-to-nothing rent I pay to my sister, and the close proximity to work, is that there is a duck park and a river across the road from our front door.

The ducks are slightly savage, especially if they suspect you have food about your person, but mostly they're adorable and in the heat of summer they spend most of their time dozing.

I'm pretty sure the low crime rate in our suburb (or at least, our street) is entirely down to these ducks. Who needs two loud barking border collies to protect their property when every passer by gets quacked at in a threatening manner?

The possibly weird thing about the duck park is that Inspector Rosenthal and I have taken to meeting here as a kind of neutral ground to discuss crime-related matters without bringing them into the house, or either of our workplaces.

It doesn't make a lot of sense, especially how often crime is also discussed in my home and workplace — but I do appreciate the lengths he goes to, to avoid me having to go anywhere near the police station.

Plus, he usually brings me a coffee.

On this particular morning, I spotted him standing on the grass with another man.

It was just after nine, early enough that the summer heat hadn't yet started creeping into the day. Still, I could tell by looking at him that Rosenthal's new friend was Not Dressed For Summer. His very nice suit (working at Fashionably Late means learning more and more about tailoring and designers) was made of the kind of heavy wool fabric that you rarely see in Australia, even in winter.

He was going to be roasting by lunch time. The way

the ducks were closing in around us, they would have eaten him by then.

"Samantha," said Rosenthal politely, passing me a hazelnut latte in a paper cup. I took it but didn't sip yet because the ducks were circling, and it didn't pay to encourage them.

"Inspector," I said, since this was clearly a work meeting, and not an Isaac meeting. "Who's your friend?"

"I'd like to introduce you to the Honourable St John Sotheby," said Rosenthal. He pronounced the first name run together, 'sinjun' which was probably correct, but he winced as he said it. All a bit too Downton Abbey for this early in the morning.

I shook hands with our murder victim's brother. "You're the one who hired Mark Harris to track your sister down, I assume?"

Rosenthal's eyes narrowed at the clear evidence that I'd been doing my research. St John Sotheby merely looked amused. And a bit like Hugh Grant in the 90s.

"No, afraid not," he chuckled. "That was my great-uncle, probably in cahoots with my brother the Viscount."

I suppose if I had a brother who was a Viscount, I'd also find ways to work it casually into conversation. I was pretty sure, however, that I could never pull off 'in cahoots'.

St John Sotheby wasn't quite what I might have imagined, if I'd given any thought to Lady Prudence/Pam West having a brother. He was posh and English enough, certainly. If you cut him, he'd bleed horse polo and Richard Curtis movies. But he was also surprisingly young — if I had to guess, I'd say somewhere between my age and forty, though his hair was carefully styled to mislead observers about whether or not he had a receding hairline.

He had a vibe about him, like he was used to being surrounded by people who laughed at his jokes and passed him martinis.

"Sorry for your loss," I offered, keeping things neutral since I had no idea what was going on here.

"So kind," Sotheby replied in his 'my-brother-is-a-Viscount' accent. "I didn't know my sister at all, as it happens. She'd already run off from boarding school when I was born — to my father's second wife. We heard she was in Australia, making films and such. One of my great-aunts kept in touch. Then, of course, she disappeared entirely, and it all became rather a bother."

Rather a bother was an interesting way to talk about losing a member of your family, even one you'd never met.

"The family all knew she was working under the name Prue Scythe?" I asked. I wondered where Rosenthal's 'not Prue Scythe' theory came in to all this.

"Oh, all the uncles and aunts said as much," said St John dramatically. "Terrible scandal, those vampire movies. Such larks. Our family barely approves of the opera, let alone the cinema. And speaking with an Australian accent her her television interviews! Quite beyond the pale. But at least one knew where she was."

He had a twinkle to him, a hint of humour beneath the unrelenting weight of aristocratic nose and fancy pants suit. A tendency towards both sarcasm and melodrama. I decided that I liked him provisionally, as long as he didn't turn out to be a surprise murder suspect.

"Why did you come all the way out here if you didn't know your sister well enough to identify her body?"

"Someone of the family had to represent," St John shrugged. "I rather drew the short straw. You know how it is, youngest sibling. Gets all the rubbish jobs. Still, Australia. Always wanted to come, meet a crocodile. Bit disappointed no one's flung a bear at my head so far, or filled my shoes with spiders." He peered at the nearby gum trees with all the justifiable caution of a man who has read memes about dropbears.

"And is she?" I pressed. "Your sister, I mean."

"Goodness, yes!" exclaimed Sotheby. "Bit grim, seeing the old duck laid out like that, but I can tell she's one of ours. We all look a bit the same, you know, the cousins and such. Only just shook off the nineteenth century tendency towards inbreeding." He guffawed a little to himself. "She's the spit of my uncle Alfie. But then, of course — the good Inspector here raised his theory with me about her possibly not being the same person as the vampire lady with the Australian accent on the television. And didn't that just put the cat among the pigeons? I can't wait to tell Great-Aunt Enid she's been tutting at the wrong person for decades."

I gave Rosenthal a very stern look indeed. "Inspector, have you gone rogue?" If I'd only worn pearls that morning, it might be time to clutch them.

"Working on it," said Rosenthal without a hint of shame. "Lyn Murphy's shut me out of the case. Wants to make sure all the gold stars go on her ledger, I suppose. Gunning for the next level job. I don't know why she's trying so hard. Everyone knows she has it in the bag."

"So what's the problem? She won't listen to your theories, so you come to me?" I was not keen on the idea of annoying any police inspector, least of all a tall scary female one who was not dating my sister, and thus had no reason to go easy on me.

"I don't care about who gets the credit," Rosenthal said firmly. "I just want to minimise the damage."

"She's already made an arrest," I pointed out.

He winced. "Well aware. And it will not make any of us look good if she's arrested the wrong man." He gave me a thoughtful look. "Do you think she's arrested the wrong man?"

"Too soon to tell," I said cagily. "There was clearly something on that phone which implicated Bry. I don't suppose you know what it is?"

Rosenthal gave me a blank look which suggested yes, he knew exactly what it was. "I know there was a lot of pressure to make an early arrest. I told her she was jumping the gun, but she seemed determined."

"So, not that I don't appreciate the coffee and the introduction," I said, wanting to wind this up quickly. The boutique might not open until ten most days, but Morgaine has been more than generous as a boss. I don't like to disappoint her by taking advantage. "But what exactly are we doing here?"

"I'd rather like to hire you," said the son of the Earl. "To find out who killed my sister, and the true story of Prue Scythe. Whether it's Bryson Carmichael or not, I want to know the truth to my satisfaction, not the court's. It wouldn't do to have any loose ends hanging."

If I'd been sipping my coffee at the time, I would have

spat it out over his designer suit. "You don't think the police are already doing that job?"

"Lyn — Inspector Murphy won't listen to me," said Rosenthal glumly.

I narrowed my eyes at him. "And you think I will." I was certain it wasn't St John Sotheby's own idea to hire me.

"I need eyes and ears on the ground," shrugged Rosenthal. "You've proven to be good at that in the past." Shameless. The man was shameless. Either Trace or I had been a very bad influence on him.

"I already have a client," I reminded him. "I mean, clients. One of them might be under arrest, but they still hired me first."

To be fair, the Carmichaels had mostly hired me to help protect Bry from the police, and I had failed spectacularly.

"This one pays in pounds sterling," said St John Sotheby, with a wide smile. "If that's helpful information at all. And I'm quite generous when it comes to expenses and the like."

I did need a new car.

"As long as you understand," I warned St John Sotheby. "I'm still only working on this part-time. And most of my expertise is in fashion, not murder."

"Doesn't bother *me*," said the son of an Earl, brother of a Viscount. "I appreciate a sense of style."

❦

"It's nearly February," mused Morgaine, towards the end of my Fashionably Late shift. The heat of the day had ratcheted up to 'brutal, verging on stinker' around lunch time, which meant no one was interested in shopping for stylish upcycled frocks. The second anyone got within arm's reach of the beach, all they wanted to buy was icy-poles and iced coffees, neither of which we sold at our particular shop. "Is Valentine's Day too obvious a theme for the front window? I can't quite face red roses and giant boxes of chocolates. Though I did enjoy last year when Paisley just made a dress of old chocolate wrappers and put the mannequin in a box…"

My mind was already on murder, which explains why I said: "Why not Valentine Noir? The mannequins can be all black widows, or mobsters trying to murder each other. While also on a date with Boris."

Boris is our only male mannequin. He's on the elderly side now, with a chipped veneer, but he's a classic. Diana, Morgaine's super glamorous, slightly-retired mother who also happens to be the owner of Fashionably Late, claims she stole Boris from a department store in London in the 1970s, and brought him with her on the plane.

He does look a bit like a groovy Ken doll, so the story tracks. Like all of Diana's wild 'back in the day' stories, the world feels better when you believe they really happened.

"Love it!" said Morgaine, clapping her hands. "Valentine's Day Massacre, with lots of red hankies and satin lingerie spilling everywhere instead of blood. I'll need you to do a dye batch before the weekend." She started sketching ideas on the back of what might be the rates bill.

"By the way, I gave Paisley the afternoon off. You're welcome."

"Why?" An innocent enough question, which was immediately answered when the most extraordinary vehicle pulled up in front of the boutique.

It was a tiny hatchback, bright orange and covered in decals that made it clear the previous owner (or possibly the current owner) was deeply committed to a Pop Art aesthetic. It was like Andy Warhol had sneezed in a birthday cake factory. Marilyn Monroe's face was sprayed on the roof — inexpertly, though impressively recognisable. There were polka dots and swirly spirals on the paintwork. The two front seats were covered in faux furs that looked like they'd been stripped off a unicorn.

Oh, and there were L plates on the front and back.

Paisley, wearing purple sunglasses and a fluffy purple hat (at a guess, I'd say a Disney monster had been hunted and skinned to make it), waved at me from the front seat.

"They need to get their hours up," said Morgaine, not looking up from her Valentine Noir preliminary sketches. "And I hear you have some kilometres to travel this week."

Well, yes. It was a good half hour over the mountain road to the Huon from here, a bit longer in busy traffic. Trace needed her own car today, in order to sell houses and pay our bills.

"Do you secretly organise everyone's lives behind their backs to create maximum efficiency?" I asked Morgaine, rightfully suspicious.

"Only my employees! Off you go. Have a nice drive."

Learner drivers in Tasmania need to log something like a gajillion supervised hours driving before they can go for their practical test. I didn't have transport of my own. This plot of Morgaine's and Paisley's would solve more problems than it caused.

Hopefully.

Luckily, Paisley's driving technique was more akin to their calm handling of a sewing machine than it was similar to their habit of flailing while talking, so the drive down to Wee Goat Farm wasn't too exciting.

I was at least able to run through what I'd found out so far — the surprise team up of Inspector Rosenthal with a son of an Earl, the many pen-names of P West, and the discovery of what Paisley persisted in calling the murder scarf among the abandoned suits of Grandfather Carmichael, deceased.

"So," said Paisley as we pulled up and over the peak of the Huon Highway, a road that is also a mountain. "We think the Viscount's the murderer, right?"

"The Viscount is still in England," I protested. "That would be quite an achievement, to murder by proxy."

"Oh, I was accusing the other brother. The one that's here. Richard E Grant."

"*Hugh* Grant. Also, he was not in the country at the time of the murder," I said firmly.

"But Harris works for their family, right? He could be, like, their murder butler."

The good thing about having Pais around was, it always made me felt like the sensible, level-headed one.

"Firstly, that's not a thing, and secondly, we already know Harris is a private detective. A real one."

"We're a real one," Paisley said, sounding offended.

"I mean, we're not," I corrected them. I had looked up the state requirements of a private investigator while I was at work today, slightly worried by the official feeling of the retainer cheque that St John Sotheby had handed me — it had three zeroes in it, and the third one was making my impostor syndrome twang a guilty tune.

Being asked to upcycle some old suits into chair cushions while discreetly asking some nosy questions of murder suspects was one thing. But now I had a genuine English gentleman as a client, and a police inspector endorsing me. Surely I needed more than a card in a dress shop window to count as a proper detective... right?

As it turned out, yes. In Tasmania, you need to meet certain guidelines and do a government test to be licensed as a private investigator. You don't need formal investigative experience like in other states... but you do need a clean criminal record.

That was the part that was stressing me out most. I hadn't been convicted, of course. But my arrest and trial would show up, surely, if anyone searched my name on a police database. That was the reason I still avoided volunteering at Daisy's school, though she and Trace had asked many times if I'd like to. You need a police check for volunteering around kids. Somehow, I didn't think bringing in my family's favourite police inspector and saying 'this one thinks I'm okay' would cut the mustard.

It was something to think about. Private investigator. Was that something I wanted to be? Or was I going to just

tiptoe back to my rare Bolivian buttons and avoid the
chaos and stress of another police investigation?

Clearly, I was going all in for investigation. How else
could I explain driving down once again to the Huon
Valley?

"Sam," Paisley interrupted my thoughts. "What's going
on over there?"

While I was musing away, we had arrived at the turn
off to Wee Goat Farm, where the dirt track disappeared up
over the hill. Paisley had stopped the car by the letter box
to stickybeak at what was happening in the lower paddock.

A few trucks had pulled up on the grass, along with a
plain clothes police car I recognised. Inspector Murphy
stood on the grass in her sensible shoes (no teetering heels
for her, she made good choices in the workplace). Some
farmer type was getting up in her face, arguing loudly
while she did her icy 'you don't scare me, I can arrest you'
thing of which I was terrified, while also being a bit
envious.

I don't think I've ever in my life made anyone scared
just by looking at them. Surely that's a convenient life skill
to have in your back pocket.

"What's happening here, then?" Paisley asked again.

I had no idea.

To my surprise, Bry Carmichael got out of the back
seat of the Inspector's car, walking slowly towards the
argument with his arms spread in 'watch me charm my
way out of this' body language which surely wasn't going
to end well.

"We should go up to the house," I said nervously.
Inspector Murphy looked like she was about to arrest

everyone in sight, and I didn't have it in me to be part of that.

"You're no fun," Paisley pouted, but drove the little orange car up the rickety driveway, towards the house. "As you are the supervising driver, I guess I'll do what you say."

I wish that worked more in real life.

13

REESE CARMICHAEL WAS A STRESS BAKER.

Paisley and I parked next to the police car on duty at the farm house, greeted by the usual friendly barking of Chilli and Bandit. A red-faced Reese stuck his head out the kitchen door, saw it was us, did a slight double take at the sight of Paisley's frankly astonishing car, and then retreated back into the kitchen.

The police protection detail today consisted of Sergeant Deng and a younger officer I didn't recognise.

"Samantha," Deng said politely. "How are things?" Coached by Rosenthal, I thought, in being as unthreatening as possible.

"You know your boss is in the front paddock, fighting with the locals?" I asked.

Deng winced a little. "Well aware," he said.

"You don't think we should go and help her?" the other officer asked him, shooting me a suspicious look.

"Don't get distracted, Constable Craig," sighed Deng. "We have a job to do right here."

"Eating cakes all day is not our job," muttered the constable.

"No need to be sour because of your dietary restrictions, Constable."

Paisley brightened. "There are cakes? What kind of cakes?"

The kitchen door slammed again. Reese came out, looking like thunder. He was holding a plastic tupperware full of what looked like quality patisserie.

"Eclairs and macarons," he said in the grumpiest tone imaginable, shoving the tupperware at Sergeant Deng. "Trying out different flavours."

"Excellent," said Deng, delighted.

"The macarons are dairy and gluten-free," Reese said abruptly to Constable Craig, then turned around and went back into the farm house.

"Thank you," said Constable Craig belatedly, sounding a bit stunned.

"Macarons!" yipped Paisley, darting in the direction of the kitchen.

I walked at a more sedate pace.

By the time I made it inside the kitchen, Paisley already had their mouth full of macaron.

The table looked like a french cafe had exploded, prettily. Several kinds of cake and pastry in small batches: cherry danishes, tiny choux buns with custard, some kind of fancy swirled shortbread, rhubarb friands and golden madeleines. Plus the chocolate eclairs and four different colours of macaron.

"Were you up all night?" I said, startled by the sheer range of it all.

"Something like that," Reese muttered, passing Paisley the macaron plate. "The purple ones are lavender and thyme, grown locally," he added absently.

Paisley took two.

"No idea where my galah of a brother is," Reese added, sounding sour. "There was supposed to be a bail hearing this morning. Mum said the lawyer would handle it and I didn't need to come up. But I've heard nothing. How did they even have enough to charge him? What did he *say*?"

"He's down in the lower paddock," I said as soon as I could get a word in edgewise, taking a seat at the table. "Can I have a macaron?"

Reese shoved the whole plate in my direction — I had to grab it or let it fall. "The pink ones are strawberry and wasabi. What do you mean he's in the lower paddock?" He swung around immediately, as if looking for the keys to his truck.

"Don't go down there," I warned. "There was some kind of altercation with the locals. And Inspector Murphy. I guess she's giving him a lift home? All very civilised. I'm sure he'll be here in a minute."

If I distracted myself with enough pretty cakes, maybe the words 'bail hearing' wouldn't clang so harshly in my brain. My own had been awful: I'd been lost in a haze of shock and numbness by that point. I genuinely thought they might be planning to keep me in custody for weeks, or months…

Bry had got off lightly, it seemed, bailed out in less than 24 hours with a lift home thrown into the bargain.

"That inspector had better not be pissing off the

locals." Reese blew out a breath. "Bad enough that this murder investigation keeps dragging on. If they put a stop to the goat race, it will be a disaster. We might as well close up shop. No one around here ever forgets *anything*."

"Are these cakes for the goat race refreshments tent?" I shifted a few things around so I could put down the plate of macarons.

"I have to go," said Reese, finally finding his keys and shoving them in a pocket. "Sort this out."

"Don't get arrested!" said Paisley. "OMG Sam, you have to try one of these tiny fluffy custard balls."

Almost as soon as Reese was out the door, we heard Bandit and Chilli barking, loudly, then the familiar clattering sound of wheels on gravel.

"Yeah," said Paisley thoughtfully. "There's no way anyone snuck on to this property the night of the murder."

"Unless one of the dogs did the strangling," I mused.

"Sam! How dare you suggest those beautiful dogs wouldn't work as a carefully honed assassination unit. They'd have managed to hide the body better."

In the yard outside, the police were all keeping their distance while Reese and the two dogs welcomed Bry back.

Inspector Murphy did not look happy. "I suppose you're responsible for those people on your property?"

"Jack and Dave," Bry said in an undertone.

"Right," said Reese. "Yes. They're supposed to be there. Setting up for the big goat race on Sunday."

"Wee Goat Race," said Bry, who looked tired but happy to be home. "Get the branding right, mate."

Reese rolled his eyes. "Get inside. I bet you're starving."

Bry moved away from his brother, but made it no further than the verandah, dropping to the step near me and Paisley so that Bandit and Chilli could love him more effectively.

Those were two very happy dogs.

"You were told to limit who came on to your property," Inspector Murphy told Reese sternly. "This is still a crime scene."

Reese sighed. "*This* is a working farm, Inspector. And no, we weren't told to limit who came on the property. We were told that our guests in the cottages weren't allowed to leave. And how long exactly is that going on for, by the way?"

"As long as Tasmania Police requires it."

"Tasmania Police didn't say anything about disrupting an established event on site. Our two lower paddocks are about as far from the crime scene as you can get without leaving our land. The permits for the goat race event were filed months ago. Traffic and parking is sorted. Catering and power, sorted. Temporary toilet facilities will be delivered tomorrow. The sign advertising the event has been there since before this murder took over all of our lives. I promise no member of the public will be coming up to the farm house, to the cottages or the crime scene during the event, which will be contained to those two paddocks down on the main road. If you're planning to cancel one of our most popular local community gatherings, I'd prefer you inform the mayor yourself. She's an old friend of my mother's and I don't like to disappoint her." Reese took a deep breath, probably a bit light-headed from name dropping his family connection with the mayor so hard.

Inspector Murphy looked unimpressed. "Are you done?"

"That depends on whether getting sarcastic with the police is an arrestable offence," said Reese, looking slightly ashamed of himself.

"We usually call it obstruction of justice," Murphy said with one eyebrow raised.

See, she was terrifying, but every now and then she pulled out something quite human and sassy, and I started almost liking her.

We all hung around awkwardly while Inspector Murphy consulted with Sergeant Deng, who had sensibly managed to stash his supply of patisserie. His new boss was not the sort to be sympathetic about scoffing a cheeky eclair or two while on the job.

"The event can go ahead," Murphy said finally, reluctantly, returning to Reese. "We will cordon off the rest of the farm to ensure no members of the public cross into our area of interest."

"Thank you," said Reese, sounding faintly surprised. "I appreciate it. And I'm sure the mayor will, too. She's a big fan of tiny goats."

"As the householder," Inspector Murphy went on. "I am obliged to inform you that we have extended our warrant for a further search of your property."

Ah. That explained the apparent concession about the goat race.

"Where do you plan to search?" Reese asked.

"Everywhere. Again. Ms Sullivan's discovery of the scarf showed that the previous searches were either lacking, or that one of our suspects has been moving evidence."

Inspector Murphy handed over the print-out of the warrant.

"Fine," said Reese, after reading it over. "Please send a copy to our lawyer. But I have new guests due to come in next week. I've cancelled previous bookings for this weekend. I want to have our current guests out of here by Monday. If you want to keep them in the area, you can put them up in your own spare room."

"That's fair," said Inspector Murphy calmly.

"And I'd like to be present for any search around the livestock, to make sure it's not too disruptive. Duckula and Lestat have been off their milk since this whole business started."

"That's entirely reasonable."

"Okay then."

They looked at each other for a moment, then Reese turned and headed into the house. Bry, the dogs, Paisley and I all followed him in.

"Looking back," Paisley told cheerfully. "You really should have name-dropped the mayor, like, five days ago."

"We live and learn," said Reese.

"Wow," said Bry, staring at the table full of fancy cakes. "When you volunteered us to do the cake stall at the race, mate, I was thinking lamingtons. Maybe a sponge."

"Didn't sleep well," said his brother shortly. "I put your phone on the charger. Go call Mum, let her know you're home. She's been worried, since she wasn't able to get to the bail hearing in person. I'd have been there anyone told me when it was," he added. "Who even paid your bail?"

"Mum's friend Diana paid it," said Bry, grabbing a chocolate eclair from the selection. "Classy lady. Offered to cover the lawyer's costs, too. I'll call Mum, but I am eating this while I talk." He disappeared upstairs.

"You and I have to talk too, mate!" Reese called after him.

"Can't hear you, eating!"

The three of us stared at the display of cakes and cream.

"I get that this is a way of showing off your fancy-schmancy goat milk products," said Paisley. "But isn't all this whipped cream going to like, melt in the sun? The forecast for Sunday is high with a side of bushfire smoke."

"We have a fridge on the back of the ute," said Reese. "But yeah. You're right. Should have just made lamingtons. Everyone likes lamingtons."

Paisley shrugged and started helping put the leftovers into the large tupperware containers that had been left to dry beside the sink. "We've all been there. Insomnia and crafting is a bad combination. I once made a three piece suit out of an old doona cover while binge-watching all of Game of Thrones over a weekend."

"I once planned a C-list celebrity wedding with three days notice," I offered. "Afterwards I had to have a caffeine detox."

"I wasn't rude to the inspector, was I?" Reese asked

suddenly, holding a container of macarons. "I think I blacked out there for a minute."

"It's fine," said Paisley. "I'm sure high-ranked police officers who've broken through the glass ceiling and punched the patriarchy in the face to get where they are almost *never* hold grudges."

~

After a long conversation with his mother, Bry came back downstairs and settled in a large recliner chair in the shady living room, with both dogs happily lolling at his feet.

Reese made tea for everyone, and allowed himself to be lightly pushed at a couch in order to finally get off his own feet.

"Where are we at with the investigation?" asked Bry, bright-eyed.

"Let's start with you," said Reese evenly. "What the hell happened?"

"I got arrested, didn't I?"

"Yeah, I figured that much out. How? Why? You were only taken in for questioning."

"They didn't like my answers!" Bry grouched. An odd sort of look crossed his face. "Also, I kind of lied to them. Early on. Didn't go down well."

"*Bry.*"

"I know, okay? Mum already gave me a serve about it. I took it back like, right away. That was before Enright turned up, the lawyer. Thanks for sending her to me, mate," Bry added to his brother.

"That wasn't me, it was Doone," said Reese. "Our

estate solicitor," he explained to the rest of us. "I asked him if he could recommend a criminal lawyer fast and he got his niece on to it."

"Anyway," Bry went on. "They'd already been at me for an hour and a half when Enright turned up. I'd made a mess of it. She was a champ, had my back all the way. That inspector kept leaving, coming back, asking the same questions over and over, didn't like the answers any better. Enright eventually said they'd have to let me go if they had nothing to charge me with."

"And?" Reese looked hunted.

"They charged me with making a false statement, didn't they? So they could keep me overnight. But I still didn't give them what they wanted about the other stuff." Bry looked at me. "That scarf business didn't help, Sam! I had no idea what was going on when they started asking about that."

"Sorry," I said automatically.

"Nah, you're good. Just wasn't the best timing for me. One more thing to be confused about."

"Wait." Reese rubbed his forehead in a stress headache kind of way. "So you weren't arrested for the actual murder?"

Bry looked horrified. "No! Is that what you thought?"

"That's what —" Reese turned to me. "She made it sound like that, yeah?"

"She definitely did," I agreed. "Probably wanted to rattle you."

"It worked."

"They brought me in for questioning again this morning. Inspector Murphy was trying to get me alone without the lawyer, I reckon. I wouldn't speak without Enright, so the whole thing took us almost the whole way to my bail hearing." Bry looked exhausted. "Good news is they won't be allowed to question me again like that unless they find more evidence against me, because they went over their maximum time. And there isn't any. Evidence, I mean."

"They're searching for something," said Reese darkly. "Again. Like they haven't already combed this place twice."

"Yeah, I overheard Murphy talking to one of her junior officers at the station. They're hot on finding some digital camera Pam had. The inspector is convinced whatever's on there will give her all the evidence she needs to stick me with a murder charge."

"And what's on the camera?" Reese asked levelly.

Bry gave him a filthy look. "Oh, thanks very bloody much. I thought at least you'd be on my side."

"I'm always on your side."

"As long as I haven't killed anyone." Bry's face was tight.

Investigation or no investigation, I was starting to feel like Paisley and I shouldn't be here for this.

"They called me in because there were a bunch of photos of me on Pam's phone, okay?" Bry blurted out a moment later. "That's it. The big mystery. I was stupid enough to act like I didn't know about them for the first ten minutes of the interview, which got me stuck with the false statement charge. Enright reckons she can get it turned over in court because I never signed a false state-ment, and she's gonna push hard on me being a complete

idiot who got confused about due process." He gave a
weak smile and two thumbs up.

Reese's expression was a picture. "What kind of
photos?"

"Shirtless pics," Bry muttered.

"Well, now it's getting interesting," said Paisley,
leaning their chin on their hands.

"It's not what you think!" protested Bry.

"Stop telling me what I think!" snapped Reese. "Just
— tell us what's going on and why the police are so hot to
arrest you. I can't take the stress of *wondering*."

"Look, it's nothing weird," said Bry. "It just looks
weird. Pam wrote all those books, right? And a bunch of
them she published them herself. She said she made more
money that way. Indie publishing. Her artist was always
looking for unique cover stock. She had a new series, paranormal romance. And she wanted someone to pose for
like, monster boyfriend covers. She was gonna pay pretty
well. We need new fences, so I thought, why not?"

Reese blinked. "You're going to be on romance
covers?" he said steadily.

"Paranormal romance," Bry said defensively. "It's like
— romance but with zombies and vampires and shit. Only
I'm not now, am I? Because she died."

"Right."

I had been doing some research on the kinds of books
Pam wrote, and I had a bad feeling about this. "These
shirtless pics. Were they just you? Were you holding
weapons? Threatening props?"

Bry winced. "There were a few with the chainsaw. And

a spade, which she said they could Photoshop to be like, swords or axes. Oh, and there were some with an axe."

Reese let his head fall gently to the table. "There are shirtless pics of you holding an axe on a dead woman's phone."

"Seriously," said Paisley, impressed. "Good job on not getting arrested for *murder*. And on getting yourselves a very good lawyer."

"Anyway, it's all done now," said Bry. "I talked it through with them in the end. Murphy doesn't believe me, but there's not much she can do. The photos are circumstantial. They can't prove anything about that bloody scarf, either. No idea what galah shoved it in with Grandad's suits."

"So, we're okay?" Reese said. "Apart from you having to go to court for lying to the police."

"Briefly lying out of sheer panic," Bry assured him. "Don't know what that Inspector Murphy's problem is, mate. She's convinced if she can find Pam's video camera, it will give her more to go on. But Pam never filmed me. I held the camera for her like once when she was practicing the intro for her documentary, but that's it. No compromising footage exists, so no compromising footage will send me to jail — the end."

He finished with a flourish, looking pleased with himself.

We all looked at him.

"Say that again," I said faintly. "About how Pam was filming a documentary."

14

THE POLICE ONCE AGAIN SPENT THE AFTERNOON SEARCHING
the Carmichael farm. They turned over the cottages, the
garden, the chicken coop, the goat shed (with stern super-
vision by both Carmichael brothers), the bushy acreage
and the creek.

They had at least twelve officers on site, which
suggested a certain amount of budget freedom.

It was intense, and it was scary. There wasn't a lot of
time to talk — not that I had any particularly searching
questions to ask anyone.

The remaining guests from the cottages came down to
the main house, all of them put out by the intrusion —
well, Annie and Guy looked put out. Harris, as ever,
looked distant and faintly annoyed, but that seemed to be
his default state.

Paisley at least got him into a conversation about
Priscilla, Queen of the Desert, which Harris had reluctantly
watched from the farm's select DVD library since the last
time they had their discussion of Australian films. Even

more reluctantly, he appears to have enjoyed it, though he claimed to have liked The Dish more.

I suppose there was little else to do around here with them confined to the property.

The police searched the goat shed first, followed by the shady paddock where most of the goats were currently dozing through the hot day. Harris — who had not shared whether or not he had found anything in that shed himself — watched them like a hawk, from a distance. Once the areas for the livestock were clear, and the police moved on to the cottages, Reese and Bry returned to the verandah with the rest of us.

There was homemade lemonade, cold beer, and sandwiches. I can think of worse ways to spend a hot afternoon, but I could have done without the occasional glimpse of a uniformed officer amongst the scenery.

Paisley, who had given up on getting film reviews out of the stoic Harris, moved on to Annie and Guy Archer with a fake social interest that looked remarkably genuine. Neither Annie or Guy were in the mood to be friendly, though they both had more patience with Paisley than they had for each other.

"All your touristy visits and day trips," Pais said encouragingly. "Come on. You must have a favourite thing you did on your holiday."

Guy launched into a pontificating ramble about the day he went on the boat out to MONA, the infamous Museum of Old and New Art that had become such a cultural hub in Tasmania. He, of course, was far more interested in telling everyone how the art wasn't real art, and most of it was the sort of thing he could do in an afternoon, but he seemed reasonably impressed with some of the larger, more news-worthy installations.

Not as impressed, of course, as he was with himself for going in the first place. He'd had more than a few beers on the cruise there and back, which added a sort of hazy detail to the day. I was starting to wonder if he'd seen any of the art at all, or just napped until it was time to come back.

"How did *you* like MONA?" Paisley broke in to ask Annie during a rare pause in Guy's monologue about what a great art lover (and art hater) he was.

"Oh," said Annie, with a small smile. "I didn't end up going. Funny thing. I was supposed to meet Guy at the wharf, and…"

"She missed the boat!" Guy guffawed. "Hilarious. Got her times mixed up. I wasn't going to miss out, was I?"

I opened my mouth to point out that the boats out to MONA went pretty regularly, then saw Annie's face and closed my mouth.

"So, what did you do?" Paisley pressed.

"Oh, I had a lovely time," Annie said, jiggling a little with remembered happiness. "Visited a cafe, wandered around and looked at the shops. Just the sort of day I like."

"Waste of bloody time," Guy boomed. "That's what you get for missing the boat!" He chuckled to himself.

Annie looked quietly smug. "Does anyone want more tea?" she asked brightly, and went into the kitchen.

I followed her. "I take it you didn't miss the boat by accident?" I suggested, as she put the kettle on.

Annie rolled her eyes. "Oh, Guy was being *awful* that day, I just couldn't stand another minute. Do you know, he kept insisting we were being followed? As if anyone would be interested in his silly old dry-cleaning van. What does he think, there are corporate spies wanting to get hold of his bleaching secrets?"

"Followed," I repeated, washing a few mugs in the sink to make it look like I had a purpose other than asking nosy questions. "Why would he think that?"

"That's what I said! He kept going on about it. A black car, and a woman in sunglasses, like those aren't very common things. No one even knows us in Hobart! Anyway, I had a lovely day on my own." She sighed wistfully, thinking about it. "Honestly, I think we might have been happier on separate holidays."

I thought she would probably be happier if she divorced her husband, but it wouldn't pay to distract her.

"Guy was just saying that the MONA trip was the day before Pam died," Paisley said loudly, when Annie and I returned to the verandah. "Weird, eh? How quickly things can change."

"That must have been the day after I delivered the dress," I mused. "What were you doing that day, Mr Harris? Any nice day trips for you?"

The older man turned his steely gaze on to me. "I was birdwatching," he said in his rolling Northern accent.

"Here on the farm?"

"No."

"See any good birds?"

"Several."

I had no follow up questions about birds.

The night before the day in question, that was when Annie said that Pam and Harris had some kind of video camera related conversation. Presumably the police had asked him about it. And they were still looking for the camera, or Bry would have heard all about it in his police interview.

It was so hard, trying to find the spaces between what the police might already know, without knowing everything that they knew.

Maybe Harris should be the one investigating this. Assuming he wasn't the murderer himself. He had known Pam, or her original family at least. And St John Sotheby, Pam's brother, did not seem to trust him an inch.

"I don't suppose any of you remember if Pam herself left the property that last day?" I asked casually.

Not casually enough; Harris gave me another steady glare like he was thinking *I know what you're up to*. Ha, joke was on him. That made one of us.

"I don't think so," Reese said.

Bry shook his head quickly.

"She would have been typing all day I expect," said Annie, still keeping up the illusion in public that she hadn't disliked the dead woman. "Such a hard worker!"

"Okay, so I have a weird question," I said after a thoughtful moment.

"As opposed to all your other questions?" Harris said coldly.

Fair point.

"Did any of you help Pam with a sewing project? Altering her dress. It was altered, I think, some time that day. Or night," I added, to make it clear I wasn't leaving Guy or Annie out of the equation.

Annie was the one likely to have sewing skills — not to be sexist, but it was rare to find men who knew what to

do with a sewing machine. On the other hand Guy was a
dry cleaner, and that often included industrial sewing
jobs… at the very least he should be able to hem a pair of
curtains.

All three of the cottage guests shook their heads,
looking blankly at me.

"None of you saw her with sewing supplies at all?" I
pressed.

This was ridiculous. The dress couldn't have altered
itself. One of these three — no, one of these five people
were lying. I needed to find out who.

That was when I decided to enact my brilliant, terrible
idea. The one I'd had in the middle of the night, then
dismissed, then re-entertained. The whole reason I had
borrowed a pair of recently-dyed lace-edged gloves from
the shop that morning, and stuffed them in my pocket
before coming down here today.

I hadn't been sure I would even get the opportunity to
do it, but now the police had dropped one in my lap.

When Reese went into the kitchen to find more food to
offer the guests, I dragged Paisley into the kitchen with me
after him. "We have to search the cottages," I hissed. "The
other guest cottages — the Man Cave and the Love
Shack."

I was letting Reese in on this, despite him being one of
the five potential suspects, because he'd already heard my
dress alteration rant, and I needed his help to get this
done.

Paisley looked delighted. "Detective work! About time, Sam."

Reese looked startled. "The police are literally doing that right now. Again. What do you think you'll turn up that they won't?"

"They're not looking for the same thing I am," I said firmly.

"Which is?"

"Evidence of who helped Pam alter the dress."

Reese groaned. "You're still on about that?"

"It's a missing piece of the puzzle. She needed access to a sewing machine. She's the only person who didn't leave the farm the day before she died, and she didn't use the sewing machine here in the house. Someone helped her."

"Is it relevant to her murder?"

"I don't know!" The fact that no one would admit it made it feel relevant. It was such a stupid thing to lie about. I already knew that Harris worked for the dead woman's posh British family, Guy had gone on sneaky smoke breaks with her, and Annie had straight up disliked everything about the woman. Why didn't I know this?

"You could tell the police," Reese said, but he sounded entirely unenthusiastic about that option.

"Not *these* police." If Rosenthal was here on site, I might have told him. Maybe under certain circumstances, even Sergeant Deng. But Inspector Murphy was so set on Bry being her suspect, I didn't think she would have any interest in anything I had to say that was not clear evidence that he was a murderer. "They wouldn't be obliged to tell us anything they found," I offered as my excuse. "We have to see for ourselves."

This whole operation had to be carefully managed. Reese accomplished the most difficult part — getting everyone off the verandah where they had a full view of the lower cottages — by bringing a giant electric fan into the kitchen, and announcing it was "much cooler inside."

It wasn't, but the difference was so marginal that moving from one location to another was enough for everyone to feel like it was an upgrade.

Paisley entered full distraction mode, and Bry played along, though no one had yet filled him in on why a distraction was needed. Drinks were poured. Cakes were produced from the kitchen, along with the makings for fat sandwiches of goat cheese, salad leaves and thick-cut ham from a nearby farm that the Carmichaels traded with for their goat milk ice cream.

At least I hoped it was ham and not like, alpaca charcuterie.

Reese and I lingered until we were sure the police had moved on from the cottages to the bush acreage and upper paddocks, and then we removed ourselves on the pretext of that good old upholstery project.

It was going to be super embarrassing if I got to the end of this mystery without upholstering a single chair, but I was prepared to risk it.

15

WE LEFT THE FARMHOUSE BY THE RARELY-USED FRONT
door which faced down the hill, skirting all the way around
to avoid being seen.

The doors to all three of the cottages hung wide open,
thanks to the ongoing police search. The flyscreen doors
were closed, at least, so the cottages were spared an influx
of mozzies and/or blow flies. But leaving the doors open
for so long would heat the interiors up horribly.

We started with the Man Cave, the cottage that Bry
planned at some point to upgrade to Gentleman's Parlour.

Mark Harris had left little imprint of his personality
inside the cottage where he had been staying for more than
a week. There was an extra box of Tetley's teabags on the
counter, and a jar of something called Bovril which
sounded disgusting.

In the bedroom, which the police had not disrupted
unduly, there was a zipped suitcase on the bed. The
wardrobe looked empty.

Reese balked at searching his guest's personal belongings; I had no such compunction. I put on my gloves — I really should carry disposables around with me, but the pretty lace ones would still make sure I didn't leave fingerprints — and unzipped the suitcase.

Nothing inside was folded properly, which didn't feel like Harris given his generally meticulous appearance — clearly whoever searched and left the contents was not a devotee of Marie Kondo.

(I had to resist folding his shirts properly, that would be such a giveaway.)

"No sewing machines in the side pocket?" Reese asked, not entirely sarcastically.

"Nothing here," I admitted.

There were no sneaky sewing supplies in Harris' hire car, either. It was a hatchback, which meant we didn't need to break into it for a quick search, though it was unlocked — the police had asked for full access to the vehicles and the guests had complied.

(Guy's booming response had been that he never bothered to lock his van, and no one ever broke into it. Annie looked embarrassed, but that was the normal Guy and Annie dynamic.)

Wary of noise, we didn't actually search Harris' hire car physically, just peered in all the windows and checked the boot via the back window. No scraps of fabric, and unless it was some kind of brilliant fold-out camping version, there was no space where a sewing machine could be stashed.

We tried the Love Shack next — which, to be honest, I thought would be a more likely bet. I'd looked up their website and the Archers offered curtain alterations along with dry cleaning. That meant at least one of them had the skills. Was it Annie or Guy who had secretly helped Pam bodge a solution to her too-tight dress, and why had they lied about it?

I suppose it wasn't hard to imagine why Guy might have lied. Annie was cranky enough about him disappearing for a smoke with Pam, of course he'd keep his mouth shut around his wife if he was the one who helped with the dress.

If I'd had a chance to ask him my questions separately, maybe I wouldn't have to search the cottages. But that would involve talking to Guy on my own and I couldn't imagine anything more annoying.

At least with Reese here I was unlikely to get myself arrested, and I really didn't want to think about how that was a genuine risk right now.

Why couldn't he have told the suspects and the police I was a hired cleaner, not a fabric expert? Cleaners are allowed to go anywhere, and no one bats an eyelid. Then again, we'd already learned recently that you could be arrested for lying to the police, so it's probably for the best Reese found a useful truth instead.

Inside, the holiday cottage shared by Annie and Guy Archer looked like a bomb had hit it. I could see where an effort had been made with the decor — comfy furniture, lots of throw cushions, retro romance prints on the walls, and bright splashes of red and pink against soft greys. Nothing too cheesy.

However, with what had to be every piece of clothing both Annie and Guy owned flung about the place, it was hard to appreciate the charm.

"The police made such a mess!" I said, appalled. "I can't believe they didn't tidy up after themselves."

"Nope," said Reese grimly. "This was what it looked like last time I came in to service the rooms."

Yikes.

We searched the cottage quickly, and found nothing of particular interest.

When we headed out to try our luck with the van, Reese went very still all of a sudden, then waved me urgently around one side.

Too late, I heard footsteps on the gravel road, approaching from the crest of the hill.

Reese set out to intercept whichever officer had nearly caught us. "Constable Craig," he called out. "I was just wondering whether we could close the cottages up yet before they get too hot for our guests. Are you all done here?"

I could hear the two of them continuing to talk in low voices, far enough away from the van that I felt it was worth the risk to slide open the unlocked side door, and quietly slip inside.

I pulled the door mostly shut behind me, not wanting to draw attention to my presence with a loud bang.

In the back of the van, everything was much tidier than Annie and Guy's living quarters. It was set like a little workspace, with plenty of storage and even a fold-out table on one side.

And, yes. *There it was*. Tucked into a cubby along the wall of the van, strapped in neatly so it didn't roll around. A high end, professional sewing machine. As I leaned in closer, I could even see a tiny length of red thread peeping out.

Bingo!

Reese took ages. I heard a few noises, doors being opened and closed. No more talking, so presumably Constable Craig had returned to the search, but I couldn't be sure. I couldn't quite get up the nerve to leave the van, not without my handy protective 'person who owns the house' at my side.

I did, however, take a few photos with my phone, showing the sewing machine and the thread.

Annie or Guy (my money was on Guy) had lied about helping Pam with the dress. Now I just had to get them both (him) alone and ask why.

Assuming I ever left this van.

I froze as the door to the van slowly slid open, but it was Reese. He climbed up in next to me, placing a finger on his lips, and eased the door closed again. "Still a lot of police crawling around," he murmured. "Find anything?"

Silently, I pointed out the sewing machine and the thread.

He looked impressed. "Nice one. What now?"

I spoke as quietly as I could. "I need to talk to Guy without Annie."

Reese scooted closer to me on the floor of the van, looking serious. "You think he could have done it? The dress, thing, I mean, not the murder. But maybe also the murder?"

"Someone did both those things," I whispered. "But I still have no idea why Pam felt the need to do such a secret last minute alteration instead of — calling our shop literally half an hour away."

"Maybe it wasn't supposed to be secret, just urgent," Reese mused. "And it's secret now because —"

"Because whoever did it doesn't want us to know about it," I sighed. "Yeah. It doesn't get us any closer to figuring out how Pam's murder happened. I haven't even upholstered any chairs for you. Sorry. I thought I'd be better at this."

I could never quite work Reese out. He was so grouchy, most of the time. But here, trapped in this stupid van, with me admitting that I'd wasted his time and money, he seemed oddly cheerful.

Maybe he enjoyed watching other people fail.

"Forget the chairs," he said. "I hate the chairs. Let people bring their own bloody chairs. The first time we did the Wee Goat Race, there were no fancy refreshment tents and hired loos and all that. It was just a stupid fun picnic with locals goofing around and putting the cute goats on Instagram."

I raised my eyebrows. "As a former event planner I do support the supply of toilets. But otherwise, why not go back to the more casual version?"

Reese threw up his arms, still whispering but clearly frustrated. "Bry. And Mum. Both of them with their huge plans for hosting weddings and big public events, and turning every inch of this property into a glossy brochure with upcycled wedding chairs and LED disco floors. It just keeps getting bigger, and I'm the only one who's not on board."

This was interesting. Watching someone who wasn't me have a quiet meltdown about their life choices was always fascinating. "You don't want to host weddings?"

"I don't want to cater *weddings*," Reese said flatly. "I'm a chef, not a hotel manager or event planner. I like to cook interesting food for people to appreciate and have a good night out. Slinging 80 plates of chicken or fish to angry drunk people in formalwear is like, the opposite of a restaurant. It's crowd control with side salads. You used to work weddings, right?"

"They're not for the faint-hearted," I agreed, with a weird burst of nostalgic fondness for the old days. Slinging 80 plates of chicken to angry drunk people in formalwear was my jam.

"I hate weddings," Reese said firmly. "Turning this place into a formal venue is my idea of a nightmare. Bry wants us to take out a loan to turn the big shed in the lower paddock into a rustic events hub. I don't know what's more terrifying — if we succeed or if we fail."

"So why are you going ahead with it? You already have the Farmstay Cottages. The tiny goats, the dairy produce. That's a lot."

"You'd think that would be enough," Reese agreed sourly. "Thing is, I didn't want any of that, either."

That was a surprise. "Are you saying that this whole — beautiful farmstay haven is what you pull off when you're half-hearted?"

"Yeah, well. I was going to be a pastry chef in a city restaurant. I'd done all the prep for it, training, apprentice-

ship. The works. *That* was my future. Then Grandad died,
leaving this place in a right old state. A real mess. Mum
and Bry started sparking up all these plans to save the
farm, turn it into a modern family business. They started it
all — the work on the farmhouse, the cottages, the bloody
goats."

"Please tell me you love the goats," I begged.

He gave me a pained look. "I am not a goat fan, no. On
the whole. Have you ever tried to carry a goat? Or make a
goat stand still so you can milk it? I'm rubbish at all that.
Plus they eat everything. *Everything.* I swear Spike ate my
best spatula last week. The whole thing."

"You're spoiling my hot farmer illusions," I lamented.
"You definitely still baked the scones?"

"Hell, *yes,*" Reese said fiercely. I do like a man who is
passionate about scones. "That was how it started. I helped
out here and there. Got involved with the kitchen reno.
Started coming up to cook the guest breakfasts, when I
wasn't working in Hobart. It was nice to work with Bry
and Mum, be a team — she was away a lot when we were
kids, so, yeah. It was good."

"But?"

He shrugged, looking miserable. "But Mum started
having these funny turns. Turned out she hadn't been okay
in a long time, but she ignored it and hid it from us. We
pushed her to make a bunch of appointments, lot of tests…
and when we got the diagnosis, it was MS. Multiple
bloody sclerosis. Progressing a lot faster than any of us
wanted it to."

"Crap," I breathed.

"Yep. And pretty much the same week we found out, I

got a job I'd always wanted. High end dessert bar in Sydney."

"You didn't go?"

"I wanted to. They told me I should. But I knew if I went, either Mum would wear herself out trying to do all the stuff she's always done, plus ten percent, and Bry would be stuck dealing with everything else, until neither of them could cope any more. They'd have to sell up. And I'd feel shit about it forever."

"So you stayed."

Reese held his hands out, indicating the battered van interior. "The farm is my restaurant. And the guests do like my scones."

"You said she lives in Hobart now. Your mother."

"Assisted living unit. The last eighteen months, she started having major mobility issues, fell a couple of times. We all got scared. She organised the place in town herself. It's supposed to be temporary, just for a year or so while we improve the accessibility on the farm, but I'm not sure she even wants to come home. She's living with people she likes, she's a lot more independent than she can be here, where she's limited to the ground floor of the house. The renovations are slow going and expensive, getting everything installed to regulation. And it doesn't stop the real problem which is that when she is here…"

"She wants to work all the time?"

"Seriously, *all the time*," he groaned.

"Hosting weddings and events sounds like a lot more to add to a full plate, if you and Bry are going to be the only ones here," I said thoughtfully.

"You said it. And also — none of our businesses quite

turn enough of a profit on their own. The goats are cute but they suck up money. The B&B is only really popular five months of the year. The goat milk dairy is popular locally, especially the ice cream, but we can't produce enough to take the next step with distribution. We keep being almost sustainable. Just enough to keep hope alive. And that was before we had a murder on the property…"

He buried his head in his hands.

I patted him on the shoulder, a little awkwardly. He leaned against me, his face still hidden. This was kind of nice.

Reese took a few moments to compose himself, then sat up. "Okay. Enough about me being an idiot. What about you, Sam?"

"What about me?"

"Is this like, your dream? Solving mysteries. Finding sewing machines." He looked at me seriously, like he was interested in my answer.

I laughed a little. "I don't think so."

"It's a weird thing to do, that's all. I suppose most jobs are, if you over-think it."

Fair point.

"I like solving problems," I admitted. "For people, for events. That was always my strength. My dream was to run my own wedding business, but I did that already, and it crashed and burned in the end. You know the story."

"You wouldn't go back to it? Weddings?"

"I don't know." No one had asked me that. Most people don't talk about it at all, assuming it's a sensitive topic. Which it is, of course.

But no one goes into wedding planning if they hate

weddings. My husband's betrayal had soured my memories of the business, but it was always *my* business more than his. I poured everything into it, and I loved being good at what I did.

Maybe, someday.

"It's a very human sort of industry, the wedding business," I said finally. "Lots of emotions, lots of family drama. Lots of problems, piled on top of each other."

Reese gave me a searching sort of look. "So, perfect for you. Awful for me. But perfect for you."

I smiled a little. "I do like solving problems."

"Maybe you should join the police. Wall to wall messy problems there."

That made me laugh. "Definitely not." My therapist and I had done some great work on dealing with my anxiety around the police, but that didn't mean I was ready to put on a uniform. "The consequences for people in *that* particular industry are too high, if you make a mistake."

"Whereas solving murders…" he teased.

"Basically a hobby. I haven't solved anything, Reese."

"You will," he said, like he actually believed it. Believed in me, though I'd given him no reason to have that much faith in my skills. "Look at the police — they've got no idea what to do next. They're searching the same trees over and over, finding nothing. *You're* following an actual lead. I'd bet on you to find Pam's killer."

I leaned in and kissed him.

∼

(I know, right???)

~

It was an impulse, but I can't say it's one I regret.

If I'd been thinking clearly, if I'd made a pros and cons list on one of Trace's whiteboards, the cons list probably would have included items like:

- Five Years Younger Than Me!!
- Clearly Going Through Emotional/Life-Decision Turmoil
- Might Be A Murder Suspect
- Yes Sam, Actual Murder Suspect, I Can't Believe You're Doing This Again
- Really Good at Scones (okay, that one was on the pros list).

But kissing Reese felt good, and he responded hungrily, like he'd been waiting for me to make the first move. He hands drew me close, and as the kiss deepened, I dug my hands into his hair…

The van door rolled open at speed, with a crunching sound that rattled the van. Reese and I both jumped apart, blinking into the bright sunshine.

Inspector Murphy looked unimpressed with us both.

"Hard day's upholstery, is it?" she asked in a voice heavy with sarcasm.

Yes, well. Something like that.

16

THE NEXT MORNING WAS ALL ABOUT DUCK EGG BLUE, ONE of my favourite dyeing shades. There's nothing like lifting a slightly dingy off-white fabric to the next level. (Duck egg blue is also the same shade as Aunt Harriet's bathroom, a retro but strangely relaxing space full of bronze fittings, ceramic tiles and forget-me-not floral decals.)

I was elbow-deep in one of the reclaimed baths in the laundry out the back of Fashionably Late, chatting to Paisley via Bluetooth while I turned a whole collection of not-quite-whites into that perfect, crisp light blue.

"The trouble is," I complained. "All I keep turning up is — well, evidence crumbs. Clues and hints. Means and opportunity. But there's never a motive. None of our suspects who had access to the property on the morning Pam died had any known *reason* to kill her."

"That can't be right," said Paisley in my ear. They were working the counter at the front of the shop, very much lacking in customers this early in the morning. "They're a shifty bunch."

"A shifty bunch with no motives," I grumbled. "Bry and Pam were taking covert stock photo shots for book covers. Unless she posed him shirtless with an axe without his consent, it's hard to see how that turned into a violent altercation."

"I want it to be Guy," Paisley said. "Can it be Guy?"

"He has the physical strength, I suppose," I said dubiously. "Or bulk, at least. And he lied about the sewing machine. But why would he want to murder her?"

"He fancied her and she didn't want him. Tale as old as time. Weren't they both smokers? Maybe she nicked his last cigarette. Those things are almost as expensive as petrol these days."

"It doesn't hold," I said glumly. "You can't just make up motives. Might as well say that Annie strangled Pam because she thought Guy fancied her. Or Harris did it because the Queen told him to."

"Harris is dodgy as," Paisley insisted. "And I'm not talking about his suspect opinions on classic Aussie films from the 90s. Your baby Earl said that Pam's fancy English family sent Harris here. He checked into the same B&B and what, hung around stalking her? He's a creep."

"He's a private investigator, Pais. If he's a creep, then so are we." I didn't get a creep vibe from Harris. He seemed like someone who was all about duty and doing the right thing. Maybe he thought killing Pam/Lady Prudence was justified somehow?

I drew the last of my wet duck egg blue masterpieces out of the bath, and put them in the plastic basket, then headed out to hang them up on one of the many Hills Hoist washing lines that filled the back yard.

At least it wasn't the red dye Morgaine wanted me to use on a crate of abandoned vintage lingerie for her Valentine's Noir window. Even I would draw the line at talking about murder suspects while up to my elbows in a scarlet dye bath. That's the kind of thing that gets you starring in all the wrong kinds of viral TikToks.

"You know…" Paisley said cheekily.

"Don't start with me." I could already tell from their tone of voice that I wasn't going to like this.

"Just saying, there's one suspect on the ground that you've entirely failed to consider."

"Unless Lord Muckity Muck St John the Twenty Fourth swung on to the property by zip line, killed the sister he never knew and white-water rafted out of there on a dry creek bed, several days before he set foot on Tasmanian soil, despite also having *no motive*, I don't see how…"

Paisley coughed discreetly. "There's Reese."

Damn it. I kept forgetting Reese was a suspect. Mostly because I was trying not to blab to Paisley about our epic make out session yesterday, and how it had been interrupted by a grim-faced female Inspector who had some questions about fences that apparently only Reese Carmichael could answer.

Here I went again, picking the best-looking bloke in the vicinity and assuming that made him both innocent and part of my inner trust circle. "He also has no motive…" I said weakly.

Pais leaped in like they had a page of notes prepared. "He's been super edgy about all that flirting between Pam and Bry. He doesn't seem to like any of his cottage residents. And maybe it's not a motive, but he *found the body*, Sam. If no one has a motive, it's pretty damn significant that Reese had the best means and opportunity to not only kill Pam, but also to hide that video camera. Assuming she had it with her when she died."

"I hate it when you're right," I grumbled. I could still feel the warmth of Reese's mouth on mine. I liked him. He seemed like a great guy stuck in a rough situation.

But I can't be trusted in my judgement about trustworthy men. Look at the one I married, for a start.

"Ssh, say that again later when I can enjoy it. Gotta help a customer." Paisley broke off the call.

I kept hanging out my freshly dyed duck egg blue laundry, grumbling to myself.

"You're here early," I said about noon, when Morgaine swept into the shop with her arms full of red ballgowns, black tuxedo jackets, and several violin cases.

Honestly, the carrying capacity of that woman never ceases to astound me.

"I have window design to do!" she announced. "Also, you and Paisley get an early minute today. Diana has requested your presence."

Well, that wasn't ominous at all.

Diana Wave is a force of personality, a fashion icon, a powerful and mysterious figure who guides our lives.

She's Morgaine's mother and our boss — though in her semi-retired state she only takes part in the aspects of the Fashionably Late business she most enjoys, which includes estate sale rummaging, and occasionally swanning into the shop to spot the one item of clothing that's not up to snuff.

She's awesome and terrifying. I've learned so much from her, about fashion and people and confidence.

Did I mention terrifying?

We never ask her age. We never even try to guess. Morgaine is comfortably in her forties, and Diana is… slightly older, based on anyone's logic. Her history suggests she's far, far older than anyone can imagine. She swung in the 60s, she grooved in the 70s, and I don't know for sure what she was doing in the 80s but from the photographs displayed in the upstairs loo of her gorgeous Art Deco home, she definitely attended a lot of the same parties as David Bowie and Freddie Mercury.

Paisley was excited at our summons. I was curious. Especially that we'd been summoned together. Could it have to do with our fledgling fashion detective business?

"Darlings," said Diana at the door, sweeping back to allow us to enter her glorious potted rainforest of an entry-way. "Wonderful to see you. I love what you've done with that hat, Paisley."

I noticed for the first time that Paisley's fuzzy purple hat had a large tear… no, bite, out of the brim.

"Gonna experiment with visible mending," Paisley said cheerfully.

"Assuming there's any hat left to mend after your next visit to the goat farm," I added.

"Eh, I think Lestat needed that bit of hat more than I

did."

"Come through," purred Diana. "I have a guest who is simply dying to make your acquaintance."

"Poor choice of words, Didi!" called a cheerful female voice from the sunroom at the back of the house.

"No puns, Mel, I simply can't stand it!" Diana called back, then led the way.

She was all in white today, her Chanel-narrow frame draped in flowing layers of cheesecloth and silk. The only splash of colour was a massive scarlet acrylic statement necklace that splattered across the front of her bohemian tunic like she had experienced a dramatic paintball incident.

I was used to visiting Diana in her sunroom, a lush pot-plant-heavy indoor garden space. For summer she had erected some kind of outdoor shade across her tiny concreted back courtyard, so the sunroom transformed into an oasis of shade.

"I call it my Den of Iniquity at this time of year," she confided.

Paisley and I each ended up with a bright pink mock-tail (at least, I hoped it was a mocktail, this early in the day) on our way through the kitchen to greet Diana's guest.

She was a cheerful middle aged woman in a wheel-chair, with spiky grey hair tipped with bright red, and a heavy metal t-shirt I instantly clocked as genuine vintage, not reproduction, because I've spent too much time around Paisley.

"Great t-shirt," said Paisley, getting comfortable in one of Diana's enormous basket chair.

"We have cheese, we have grapes," called Diana, coming in from the kitchen with a spectacular platter on one arm. I assumed she'd whooshed it up from nothing by wiggling her nose, witch-style. "Buckle up and get comfortable, my chickens. We are going to spill *all the tea*."

~

"I hear you've been helping my boys out, the last few days," said Diana's friend Mel, with a twinkle.

I'd had my suspicions thanks to the wheelchair. It would be a wild coincidence otherwise. "You're Bry and Reese's mum?"

Paisley actually clapped in delight. "Epic reveal."

"I am indeed!" said Mel Carmichael, sounding smug. "You're halfway there."

There was an air of expectation. I had a thought: a wild, strange idea that wouldn't go away. But somehow, I didn't quite have the confidence to say it out loud. "You're not —"

She couldn't be. Could she?

Mel's hand, demonstrating a slight tremor, pushed up the black sleeve of her t-shirt, just enough to show that she had a tattoo on her upper arm.

I'd seen it before, in the crime scene photos of a dead woman.

"You're Prue Scythe," I said, certain now. "The real Prue Scythe."

"OMG you are!" exclaimed Paisley. "I love your movies."

"Come on," said Mel, scoffing. "You are too young to have even heard of my movies."

"Vamp Pash is timeless," said Paisley fiercely. "I have a YouTube channel dedicated to your early work: the Werewolf Island shorts, and that one Halloween episode of Neighbours you scripted in 1996 that went deeply off the rails and they never officially aired."

"Ohh, a super fan," said Prue. "Usually they're my age."

"Paisley's into vintage," I explained.

"And that makes us all feel old!" exclaimed Diana. "Honestly, Vamp Pash was five minutes ago. Did I ever tell you I had a cameo in one of the beach scenes?"

"YOU DID NOT," said Paisley in an inhuman shriek.

"You made an excellent corpse, Didi," agreed Mel. The two ladies gave each other fist bumps.

I was so confused. And yet. It was starting to make sense. Rosenthal's wacky theory about Lady Prudence was correct. "So there really were two Prue Scythes?"

"Oh, there's only one of me!" insisted Mel. "But you're partly right. Prue Scythe was a creation of more than one person. And I'm the only one left alive." Sadness crossed her face in a fleeting shadow.

"You haven't told the police who you are?"

When you know your identity has been attributed to a dead woman, you make the call. Right?

"I'm about to do that," said Mel with a rueful smile. "I believe you know an inspector who might be sympathetic to my story?"

I mean, I knew a police inspector. I couldn't promise sympathy.

∼

To his credit, Isaac Rosenthal came quickly when called, this time around. He was at his office in the Kingston branch, so not far away. And my 'how much do you want to meet the real Prue Scythe' opening line was pretty enticing.

Out of respect for Mel's mobility issues, not to mention the ready supply of mocktails, I didn't suggest moving this little gathering to the duck park around the corner.

"On duty," said Rosenthal when Diana tried to pass him one of her fancy pink drinks. His tone wasn't especially sharp. Like everyone else, he was always a little dazzled by Diana Wave.

"It's just watermelon and lime, Inspector," she purred. "Excellent for hydration. Unless you'd prefer something else? I have a marvellous Virgin Bloody Mary mix."

He shook his head, but took the watermelon drink. "This is fine."

"I have a lot to tell you," said Mel. "I hope it clears some things up."

"This isn't a formal statement," Rosenthal said, eyeing her suspiciously. "Not yet. But if you tell me anything that has implications for an open investigation, I will require you to make a formal statement at the station. Do you understand?

"Believe me, Inspector Rosenthal," said Mel Carmichael with a heavy sigh. "I've been thinking about the implications of my story for a very long time. And I'm ready to tell it all."

17

THE (REAL) PRUE SCYTHE STORY

"IT STARTED WHEN I WAS AT FILM SCHOOL IN THE EARLY 90s," said Mel. "I had a tiny flat share in Melbourne — me and Prudence. Then Caity joined us, a year later, when we ran out of money and needed a third flatmate. Prudence and I shared a room so we could sublet the other one. We were having a wonderful time: taking classes, working in the same dodgy cafe. We'd bounce creative ideas off each other. Prudence had this idea for vampire novels with a strong Australian flavour. What became the Vanity Fall books."

"OMG," interjected Paisley, sounding heartbroken. "Vanity Fall is actually dead."

"Yes, she is," Mel said sombrely. "They were her stories. She wrote every word. But Caity and I threw in a bunch of suggestions along the way. To be honest, I had the most fun creating the backstory for Vanity Fall. You know the sort of thing."

I remembered the bio. "Bareback rider in the circus, once shot a President, types every novel on a vintage typewriter with purple ink, invented the marmalade sandwich."

"Exactly! We were always doing that sort of thing. Messing around, creating stories about everything. That's how we came up with Prue Scythe. She was a shared character between Prudence and I — no, I can't think of her as Prudence, really. She hated that name. Hated her whole fancy country house history, never connected to her family. She wanted to be Australian, all the way. Her accent was stronger than mine! We had a running joke, swapping names."

"So you became Prue??" I still didn't quite have clear in my head.

"I was Pamela, until I moved in with Prudence. She hated her name so much, I shared mine — we were Mel and Pammy, from that point on. It drove Caity wild — it was our joke, you see, *our* game. She wasn't really part of it. We felt bad for her, but it didn't help that she kept trying so hard. She'd repeat our jokes, copy our mannerisms. It was a bit creepy, the way she wanted to be like us, but we told ourselves to be nice to her."

"So the Vamp Pash books were almost published under the name Prue Scythe?" Paisley wondered.

Mel shook her head firmly.

"I don't think Pammy would have liked that. Too close to her real name. She'd ditched everything else from her family. Lived in dread of them tracking her down. There was an uncle she was especially scared of, I think." Mel frowned. "We talked about Prue Scythe like she was a character in our lives — super cool, wicked older sister type. If anyone did anything bad — drinking the last beer in the fridge, spilling red wine on the carpet, whatever. We blamed it on Prue Scythe. We even got the tattoos in her honour — all three of us. When I released my first short film, I asked Pammy if I could use Prue Scythe as a professional name. I liked the idea of building a persona, something I could remove if I needed to. She said that was fine, but she wanted to change her name by deed poll to Pamela. Pamela Northby," she added to Rosenthal, who made a note of it. "I think that's still her legal name. She has so many pen names these days."

"She had a credit card in the name of P West," I noted.

"She did that sort of thing, even then. Fake IDs and the like. Any time she had a chance to take on another identity, she did it. I think she had library cards in three different names. She really didn't want her family to find her — and it was easier to hide back then. Before Google, and Facebook."

"You didn't mind her taking your name?"

Mel shrugged. "It was a fair trade. I'd never really felt like a Pamela. I liked having Prue as my public face, Mel in private."

Rosenthal spoke up, asking a rare question of his own. "Have you been in touch with Pam West all this time?"

"No, not at all. We lost track after I got married, moved back to Tasmania. I had my two boys, and then just as I was starting to look at getting back into film work, my husband shot through. I was lucky — my Dad had the farm, he didn't mind looking after the kids for long stretches while I went off to Melbourne, Sydney, on various short contracts. Then I heard about the Vamp Pash books. They were so popular. When I read the first one, I knew I wanted to make it as a film. Ahead of my time," she added with a self deprecating grin. "It was before Twilight. Everyone still looked at you funny when you suggested raising funds for vampire movies, especially here in Australia. But I was right!"

"Did you contact Pam about the books?" I asked. It felt less like a murder investigation, more like I was interviewing her for that fanzine I definitely didn't start when I was fourteen and obsessed with all things Prue Scythe.

"I had to get in touch through her publisher, and it took ages. Eventually, we met up. Talked about scripts. I pulled some grant money and sponsorship together, and Pammy ended up funding a lot of the first film herself. She was even more of a hermit than ever, just writing away in a room somewhere with her vintage typewriters, pumping out manuscripts and barely seeing anyone. She admitted to me that it wasn't just about hiding from her old family. She'd had a stalker for a few years. She'd even had to move house after a break in."

Rosenthal was making a lot more notes. "Did she ever find out who he was? The stalker?"

Mel laughed shallowly. Her hands were shaking more now. "Could I have some water? Actual water, Didi, not one of your watermelon goop drinks."

"Of course, darling." Diana Wave leaped up and went to pour water, fussing a bit around her friend.

"If this is difficult for you, we can take a break," suggested Rosenthal.

"Everything's difficult these days, said Mel, sounding

both fierce and tired. "It's fine. Just a moment or two. I want to get through this."

"So, the Diabolique Festival," Mel said, skipping ahead, past the indie success of the first Vamp Pash film, the mainstream success of the second. Her blog, the rising sales of the books. We knew all that, of course. "I went the full Prue that weekend — if I did all the makeup and hair the glam semi-goth persona, it helped with being in front of cameras. I preferred to be behind them, but sometimes you couldn't avoid a public appearance. It was ridiculously easy to be just ordinary Mel when I was at home with my kids. I swear, none of the school mums had any idea who I was. The internet was a bit less… well, you couldn't get away with it now, I suppose."

"What happened to you?" Paisley burst out. "The day you disappeared. There were so many theories."

Mel looked sombre. "Pammy was getting harder and harder to work with. She wouldn't answer calls or emails. When I could get through she sounded jumpy, paranoid. I thought perhaps she was drinking a lot, or on some kind of drugs. She failed to deliver a script for the third film on deadline, and wouldn't sign off on someone else doing it. I called her before I left the hotel for the festival. She said she couldn't talk because she had a visit from an old friend. But she'd hired a beach house nearby, same suburb as my hotel, so we could finally make decisions about Vamp Pash III. We made arrangements to meet, the next day, for breakfast. Figure out if there was a future for the franchise. I was about ready to chuck it all in if she wouldn't be straight with me."

Mel sipped the water slowly. When her arm went into a slight spasm, Diana leaned in to take the cup from her, set it to one side. "Tell them what happened, Mel," she said in the gentle voice of someone who already knew how the story ended.

Another odd, twisted smile from Mel Carmichael. "I ran into an old friend," she said, and her voice cracked a little.

"It was Caity," said Mel, when she was ready to talk again. "Our old roommate. She had a — fixation, I suppose. On Pammy more than anything. But both of us, really. Our friendship. She'd always wanted to be part of what we had together. It was all mixed up for her — Pammy's history as Lady Prudence. My persona of Prue Scythe. And now there was a moderately successful movie franchise — very successful by Australian standards — and the Vanity Fall money, from the books. She wanted in. Wanted her share. Of the acclaim, I think, as much as the money."

Rosenthal's notes were becoming a novel. I could tell he had many more questions he wanted to ask. But Mel was beginning to look distinctly traumatised.

"I thought it was a weird coincidence at first," said Mel. "Running into Caity in the literal street where I was about to catch up with Pammy. But then she led me to the house, and I realised she was part of this. She kept up the illusion that it was all some fun reunion until we were inside the house. And then I realised she was keeping Pammy hostage. Me too, the second I walked in the door. She had a gun and knew how to use it."

"Wait," said Paisley. "So you just — walked out of your hotel early in the morning. Went on foot to a nearby beach house. *That's* how you disappeared?"

"Without the makeup and the wig I was just Mel. I don't think anyone looked twice at me."

"But how did the Sydney police never find you? Afterwards. There was a huge search. Helicopters. The works."

"That's a question for them. I suppose they had no reason to look for Caity, or whatever name she used to hire the house."

"But surely when you got away from her, you could have gone to the police then?"

"I could," said Mel calmly. "But I didn't."

"Why not?"

"Because by the time we got out it had been five weeks."

"Five *weeks*?" I felt hollow at the thought of it.

Mel nodded slowly. "Caity kept us prisoner for five weeks. In this grim little basement under the beach house. It was concrete lined. No one heard us yelling. Eventually, we stopped trying. She brought food, and water. Even a bloody typewriter! She was armed, always. She handled the gun so professionally. I don't know where she learned how to do it. I guess we'd all changed in the time apart. We were terrified. We promised her anything she wanted. A new Vamp Pash script. Pammy wrote the first three chapters of a new novel, to please her. We promised her creative credit on the films, front row seats to the premiere.

Pammy even agreed to get Marnie together with Cedric instead of Carmilla in the next film."

I gasped a bit at that. "Really?"

Mel looked weary, but a little amused. "Oh, Caity *hated* Carmilla. Snarky goth princess who always survives at the end? A bit too much like Prue Scythe. Like me and Pammy, back in the day. When we saw how excited Caity was at the idea of killing off Carmilla, we realised she wasn't planning to let either of us go. No matter what we said or promised."

"How did you get away from her?" Paisley asked.

Mel looked to Inspector Rosenthal, and that was when I realised why this whole thing was sounding more like a confession than the explanation to a 15 year old mystery. My heart sank for Bry and Reese. Did they know any of this?

"Are you certain you don't want a lawyer for this?" Rosenthal asked, trying to be as fair as possible.

"I've spoken to my lawyer already," said Mel. "Abby Enright, nice girl. I booked a meeting with her, after she handled Bry's bail hearing so well. I was having a bad day — wasn't up to coming to the court or the police station in person, so she even arranged for the police to take him home. Anyway, Ms Enright advised me of her recommen-dations, after I told her my story. What to say to you. What not to say. I've kept these secrets for so long. But it's time to let it all go."

Rosenthal shrugged, motioning her to go on.

"I tripped Caity on basement the stairs. The gun went off. And Pammy..." Mel closed her eyes very tightly for a moment. "She hit Caity with the typewriter. More than once. We didn't stay to check if she was dead. But we knew she was. We just left. Walked out. There was enough money in her wallet, in the kitchen upstairs, to get us to Pammy's retreat in the Dandenongs. I stayed there for a few weeks, to make sure she was okay. She wasn't, of course. But I could tell she wanted me gone, wanted to forget everything. We made a pact not to tell anyone what happened. To let Prue Scythe be dead and gone. Pammy paid for my flight home. I haven't left Tassie since. My dad — he didn't even tell the boys I was missing. Said I had a job that went longer than expected. He managed to keep them away from the news, not that they were in much danger of seeing it. Bry was nine, Reese around eleven. They weren't exactly in the cult vampire movie demographic yet."

My heart went out to her late granddad, dealing with all that alone. I wondered if that was when he started his journey of retail therapy, obsessively collecting all those suits.

"And the story about Lady Prudence being Prue Scythe?" Rosenthal pressed. I suppose he would be particularly interested in that detail.

"That was Caity," said Mel. "She leaked it to the press during our captivity. She was obsessed with the media coverage, and threw that crumb out when it looked like they were losing interest. She would come and tell us all about it every day — what they were saying on the news, what questions were being asked. She got furious whenever some new story came along and ours faded out."

"I have a question," said Paisley. "What has any of this got to do with Pammy-Lady-Prue's murder? And why did she commission us to make a copy of your —" They gasped suddenly, bouncing up and down. "OMG DO YOU STILL HAVE THE ORIGINAL DRESS?"

"I do not still have the dress," Mel Carmichael said, very calmly. "Pammy emailed me, a few months ago, for the first time in — what, fifteen years? She said she wanted to write a book about our story. The Prue Scythe disappearance, what really happened. She wanted to make a documentary. Film interviews. Go back to all the old spots. I told her about this —" She tapped the arm of her wheelchair impatiently. "I wasn't interested in raking up old dirt. I'm too bloody tired for all that. Plus we might still have criminal charges to answer for, given Caity's death. I have too much to lose." She looked at Rosenthal. Bravery or not, I saw worry on her face.

Rosenthal shrugged, tapping his notebook with a pen. "A lot depends on what was found in that beach house at the time, and what evidence remains that any violent act was committed. Presumably your abductor's body was found at the time. Full name?"

"It was Caitlyn O'Leary when we all lived together," said Mel. "I don't know what name she was using later on."

Rosenthal nodded thoughtfully. "I'll have to look into the files, talk to some of my New South Wales colleagues. You should talk to your lawyer again, arrange to come in for that formal statement."

"Could Caity have had relatives or friends, a husband, someone who held a grudge?" I asked him.

"You mean our suspects on the ground," said Rosenthal. "I agree, it would make a solid motive. I'll have to do some hunting to find out if there's any connection between Ms O'Leary and the Archers, or Mark Harris."

Not that Mark Harris wasn't already deeply connected to the case via murder victim's family.

Paisley encouraged Mel to keep going. "So you didn't want to be involved in a documentary?"

"It was so odd," Mel went on. "I hadn't heard Pammy so excited about anything since we were working on that first film. It was tempting to say yes. But I didn't want to be in front of the cameras. I'd rather people remember Prue Scythe as she was — young, glamorous, sassy. I don't want to end up as the disabled lady on the cover of the Women's Weekly with everyone talking about how brave I am."

Personally I thought it would be no bad thing to see sassy older ladies in metal t-shirts and wheelchairs on the cover of the Women's Weekly, but it wasn't my call.

"I recommended Diana's shop to Pammy," Mel added. "I thought she wanted to make Vamp Pash costumes or something like that, not the festival dress." She shuddered. "I guess she wanted to wear it for her documentary? I can't think why she thought it was a good idea. Kind of sick, when you think about it."

"Sick?" Paisley pressed.

Mel nodded, looking pale. "My red dress. *That* dress. I brought it to the beach house that morning, bagged up — Pammy had asked me to, and I found out later that Caity made her do it. She was obsessed with that damned dress — Caity, not Pammy. She loved seeing how often it came up on the news. She even wore it sometimes, with the wig, when she came to visit us in the basement. Playacting Prue

Scythe." Mel looked away, avoiding everyone's gaze. "She was wearing it when Pammy killed her. I can't think why Pammy wanted to recreate that."

'And where does Mark Harris come into it?" Rosenthal asked.

"I don't know a Mark Harris," Mel said, too quickly.

"Tall man, grey hair, British. Manchester accent. I believe he visited you at your apartment in Hobart. Two days after the death of the victim." Rosenthal looked a lot less friendly now.

"I was under surveillance?" Mel said, sounding furious. Her right arm twitched and she laid a hand over it.

"*He* was," Rosenthal said steadily.

"I believe I do want to speak to my lawyer after all," she said calmly.

"How about we meet Ms Enright at the local station," said Inspector Rosenthal. "Easier for everyone."

And I suppose, gave him a little extra time before Inspector Murphy learned he was in the process of stealing her case.

I managed to grab a minute with Rosenthal on the pavement outside Diana's house, while he was waiting for transport to collect him and Mel.

"Are you or are you not arresting Reese's mum?" I demanded.

"I'd like to arrest her for wasting police time," he muttered. "All that soapie nonsense about gun sieges at beach houses."

"You don't think she was really held hostage?"

"I'm expected to believe a woman was killed in Sydney that same red dress, five weeks after the big celebrity hunt for Prue Scythe, and no one ever made the connection, or even put a note in the Scythe disappearance file? I very much doubt that this 'Caity' even exists."

It had never occurred to me that Mel was lying. Her story sounded so raw, so real. But I suppose Rosenthal was used to people lying to him.

"Maybe her body wasn't found until much later," I suggested. "Maybe it was never found."

Though yes, that red dress should have set off all the alarms even years after Prue Scythe disappeared.

Maybe Mel had left out the part where she and Pammy disposed of the body. Or maybe Pammy went back and did it later. I could see why it seemed farfetched.

"I'll look into it," said Rosenthal. "But I don't expect to find much to support her story. If you take the stalker roommate part out, we're left with two women. One is dead. The other went off grid and never told the police or anyone in her industry she was still alive. To hide out on a farm in Tassie. That's suspicious, Sam. Trauma or no trauma."

"Do you think *Mel* killed Pam?"

"If she didn't want Pam telling the world about their story, that's a motive for murder," said Rosenthal. Like me, the lack of motives so far must have been bothering him.

"She doesn't exactly have means and opportunity, does she?" I demanded.

"That's very ableist of you, Sam. Wheelchair users can be murderers too."

"On a slope by a creek," I said incredulously. "Even if she doesn't use the wheelchair all the time, does it really sound credible she could do it? That strangling would be her murder method of choice."

"I don't like her for this," Rosenthal admitted. "And I don't think Murphy will consider her a credible suspect either."

"No, she still thinks Mel's puppy dog of a youngest son is the murderer."

Rosenthal shook his head slowly. "I didn't give Murphy enough credit on this one. You didn't hear it from me, but it turns out she's been building a case against Mark Harris all this time. St John Sotheby gave her a statement yesterday — he's convinced that his uncle sent Harris out here as a hit man, to keep Lady P from dragging the family name into the media again. And according to Ms Carmichael in there, Lady Prudence Sotheby was hiding from her rich English family for a lot longer than fifteen years.

"That's not much of a motive."

Wow, so St John Sotheby had gone straight to the police after giving me all that faff about wanting to hire me to solve the mystery. That was hurtful.

"With a family that old and rich?" Rosenthal spread his hands wide. "It might be. Murphy is convinced Harris took Pam West's camera off the property — and that visit he made to Mel Carmichael might be crucial in proving it."

"So where do I come into this? What do I say to Reese and Bry? Paisley and I were supposed to head down there this afternoon."

For more fake upholstery and maybe a bit of light kissing.

"You don't say anything," Rosenthal insisted. "You can't. Sam, I've tried not to interfere with this detective thing you have going. But this is serious. Harris is a dangerous man. I don't want you going back to the property until all this is over."

"But I was hired for three afternoons!"

"Sam," he said shortly. "Inspector Murphy has been asking a lot of questions. About who you are, and what your ties are to the Carmichael family. I can't promise she won't arrest you just for being in the wrong place at the wrong time."

And that, well. That shut me up, didn't it.

Reese sounded confused when I told him over the phone that I couldn't come down to Wee Goat Farm that afternoon.

He sounded about ten times more confused and a lot more annoyed a few hours later, when he called back. "They took my mum into questioning? What the hell, Sam?"

"She volunteered to make a statement to the police," I said quietly. "Ms Enright's with her, the lawyer. I'm sure it's all going to be fine."

"How can you know that?" he demanded. "What do you know that I don't?"

By that point, I was the one who was annoyed. "While we're talking about not knowing things. Am I really expected to believe you didn't know all along that your mother was Prue Scythe?"

There was a long silence. Then an abrupt: "I'll call you back."

Spoilers: he didn't.

18

THAT NIGHT, WE CELEBRATED. TRACE HAD SOLD A THREE-bedroom in Margate for the approximate price of a chateau in France (house prices in Tassie are insane right now).

Morgaine turned down our invite because she was having dinner with her Mum. (I don't think I was Diana Wave's favourite person right now.)

Isaac couldn't make it. Either he was still interviewing Mel Carmichael at the police station, or he didn't want us to grill him about what she had said.

Paisley came over, somehow the only one with enough energy to chase the puppy around the back yard as yet another hot afternoon ebbed into a reasonably cool evening. Only another month of summer to go. We would survive.

Daisy flopped on a beanbag on the corner of the deck with her iPod and a large orange juice on ice, every inch the world-weary nine-year-old. Occasionally she fanned herself with a decorated paper fan.

We ate tiny food on big plates, because of Trace's habit

of stocking the freezer with re-heatable hors d'oeuvres, and turning random salad items into crudités whenever she's distracted. Since living here, I've forgotten how normal people cook. The other day, I meant to make myself a quick omelette and produced a platter of devilled eggs instead.

"You did the right thing," said Trace as we made our way through a tray of curried chicken vol-au-vents, celery curls and cheesy risotto balls, plus half a bottle of white wine. "*Fashion detective* is all very well, but if this Harris is some kind of scary Yorkshire hit man, you need to be far away. Let the police deal with him."

"I know," I said. "I do know that. It's just frustrating. I was wandering around asking stupid questions and eating scones while they were doing proper police work and getting the job done. I need to go back to buttons."

"No!" Paisley announced, skidding to a halt near us with an armful of puppy. "You can do better than buttons, Sam. I think it's time."

"Time for what?" I said, startled. My glass of chilled white wine (with an ice cube to keep it chilled) tilted in an alarming way. "What is it time for?"

"Time you took off the training wheels," said Paisley in an ominous voice. "I'm going to teach you to set a sleeve."

"No!" I protested, while Trace mock-gasped and pretended to clutch her pearls. "That's way too advanced."

"Training wheels — off!" Paisley pronounced, scooping up their own frosty drink. "Collars, too. I'm going to show you how to make collars, Samantha Sullivan."

If that didn't distract me from the disappointing fizzle-out of our latest attempt to solve a murder, nothing would.

Collars! What did she think I was, some kind of dress-making genius?

I thought that was it. I thought it was over.

The police had it sorted. Reese and his brother weren't about to be arrested, though it was possible neither of them were going to ever speak to me again now their mother was involved.

I considered telling Paisley to take the Fashion Detective sign down from the shop altogether.

But the next morning, as I left the house for work, I received a weird phone call.

There was an odd clicking sound, and then a perfectly polite voice said: "Am I speaking to Samantha Sullivan?"

"Yes."

"This is the Hobart Remand Centre."

My vision hollowed out for a moment. My whole body coiled up in white hot panic. For a moment, before my common sense kicked in, I thought that this was it. There had all been some mistake and they were taking me back.

I know that's not how it works. Believe me, I've done a lot of research on prisoners' rights over the last couple of years.

But for one horrible moment, I believed it.

Through my spiralling anxiety, I almost didn't hear what she said next.

"I'm sorry, what did you say?"

"Will you accept a call from Mark Harris," the voice said again, very calmly. "He only gets one."

Harris. For some reason, he had used his one post-arrest phone call to talk to me. Instead of a lawyer. No pressure.

"Yes, I'll accept."

I went across the road and stood on the grass by the river, my ankles surrounded by ducks, waiting.

Harris. Of the three surviving cottage guests, he was the one who actually seemed capable of killing another human being. The only unlikely part was that he bothered to use a scarf instead of his bare, probably quite capable hands.

Finally, the connection came through. "Hello, Samantha." Harris sounded as he always did. Polite, professional and mildly annoyed that he had to have any contact with people. There was no birdwatching in the remand centre.

"Why are you calling?" I asked him. "Why are you calling *me*?"

"Because I know I didn't do it," he replied. "You're smart enough to know that too. Which means you're going to keep nosing around, and maybe another woman ends up strangled in a creek. So, let me help you now, before it's too late."

"Thank you?" I ventured, feeling a bit patronised.

"We don't have long. What do you want to know?"

What didn't I want to know! "Were you really here to track down Pam — Prudence for her family?"

"Young St John's been in your ear. Yes. They hired me. They do that."

"And you always do what the family ask of you?"

"I'm not an assassin, if that's what you're asking. The Sotheby family are arseholes, but they're not 'hire a man to knock off an inconvenient relative' kind of arseholes. Well. Except Great Uncle Jolyon, but they don't let him have a bank account any more."

"Why you? Why did they send you?"

"I knew Lady Prudence a little," Harris sighed. "Back in the day. I was just a family bodyguard back then, before I started my own agency. Bright kid. Always making up stories. Caught her once painting all her Barbie dolls hair black so she could play vampires with them."

That sounded like a believable backstory for a kid who would grow up to be the famous vampire novelist Vanity Fall. Lady Prudence, I had to keep reminding myself, was the one who wrote the books, not the one who made the movies.

"There has to be more than that. If she knows you worked for her family, why wouldn't she run a mile the second you turned up here?" Assuming she even recognised him, decades later.

"I'm the one who let her get away," Harris said flatly. "She knew the family would try to stop her if she left the country. She'd just turned eighteen, was still supposed to be at boarding school for another four weeks. She paid me a lot of money to look the other way after I found out she had applied for her passport, bought a ticket to Australia."

"You don't seem like the bribe taking sort," I said curiously.

"Depends who's paying the bribe. I felt sorry for the kid."

"And so when you turned up again, she felt she could trust you?"

Harris sighed deeply. "She'd reached out to film contacts, hinting at a tell-all Prue Scythe film. One of my assistants found out about it, passed the story along. The family sent me out to pay her off. She refused at first, then agreed to bring everything to the farm. In exchange for a very large deposit in her bank balance."

Interesting. Pammy had known that she would be meeting Harris, when she arrived at the cottages. She had made the deal to give it all up... but had still gone ahead with filming new footage, involving that dress.

"So, you have the camera now?" I asked.

A long pause. "It was destroyed. The day before Lady Prudence's death."

"And the contents?"

"The family wanted proof I had destroyed it. I sent them the remains by international post."

"You can't prove you've destroyed digital content. You could have backed it all up first. *Pam* could have backed it up first."

"Oh, I never would have thought of that," Harris said in that everything-is-sarcasm voice of his. "My employers are elderly, entitled aristocrats. I did not choose to point out to them that their conditions for passing over the money were unrealistic. I followed those instruction to the letter. I retired next month. This was my final service to the the Sotheby family."

"And you deposited a significant amount of money into an account for Pam — for Lady Prudence?"

"I did. Under her legal name. Pamela Northby. She provided the account details herself."

"Did her great-uncle not consider that giving someone a huge amount of money to not make a film is … potentially just funding her next film?"

"Did I not mention that I retire in three and a half weeks?" Harris said impatiently. "They're about to wind up this call, Samantha."

"What else do I need to know?" Clearly there was no time to play detective games.

A very brief pause at his end. "Lady Prudence had a second phone. Red cover. I saw her reading texts off it once, looking upset."

"A second phone?" The police had only found one. "Did that get destroyed with the video camera?"

"Nothing to do with me," Harris said calmly. "But on the night she came to my cabin for our financial exchange, she asked me if I'd sent it to her before I arrived."

"Someone sent her a phone."

"Not only the phone," he said. "She also asked if I sent her a dress."

19

THE FIRST WEEK OF FEBRUARY IS THE END OF THE SUMMER holiday for kids and teens across the state. In the Fashionably Late calendar, that meant dozens of teenagers in the Kingston area finally getting around to trading in their formal outfits from school leavers.

They arrived in bunches, carrying suits with stained sleeves, sweaty satin cocktail gowns and shoes that had almost certainly been thrown up on. Nearly every kid who invested in a floor-length gown had managed to rip it when someone else trod on their hem.

Morgaine loves this time of year. I think she enjoys it even more than when she gets to sell the original moderately priced formalwear in November.

"Ooh, purple shot satin," she said in delight as one slightly foxed ballgown made its way back in. "I remember this one."

"No cash, only credit!" Paisley yelled from the workshop.

"I'll give you ten if you want cash," Morgaine said immediately. "Thirty in credit."

"I paid two hundred for it," wailed the teen.

"You paid me sixty, three months ago," Morgaine replied. "And it didn't have that fruit punch stain on the neckline."

While I was hanging the punch-stained shot satin out back, along with a tailored evening jacket with Spider-Man print lining which had suffered a catastrophic salsa verde explosion (at least, that's what I hoped that stain was), I got a text from an unknown number.

Hey Sam, this is Bry. Hope you don't mind me getting in touch.

Of course I don't mind, I texted back quickly. **How are things at the farm?** (Is Reese still mad at me?)

Even in the midst of Formalwear II: the Sequel, I had been thinking a lot about them over the last few days. In a short space of time, I'd got rather attached to their lovely farm house and verandah… and the cute tiny goats…

And, okay. Some of the people also didn't suck.

Sorted! Bry texted me. **Harris was arrested. Guy and Annie are packing their van — I convinced them to stay for the Wee Goat Race, but they'll be back to Launnie soon enough. New guests roll in on Tuesday.**

I'm glad it all worked out, I sent back.

Hopefully once everything settled down, Reese would have the guts to have a talk with his brother about the family business. I hated to think about him continuing to make all those sacrifices, being miserable. Not that it had anything to do with me.

We appreciate your help, Bry said now.

I wondered how inclusive the 'we' was.

Is everything all right with your mum? I tried.

This time there was a whole ten minutes before he sent the next text. **All good. You'll come for the race, won't you? Kicks off 10am Sunday. Bring Paisley.**

I probably shouldn't, I texted.

On the other hand, if the case was over, why shouldn't I? I'd kept my word to Rosenthal and stayed away from Wee Goat Farm until Harris was arrested. Did I have to stay away forever?

Sure, I wasn't convinced they had the right man in Harris. He might indeed be a diabolical mastermind, dropping all those clues and hints about Pammy/Lady Prudence in the hopes I would… well, what was his motivation for making up what he said on the phone? To confuse me?

The revelation that the murder victim had not ordered that red dress for herself was driving me batty. I couldn't stop thinking about it. A tidal wave of makes-no-sense.

Who would send Pam that dress, and why? To remind her about what she and Mel had done to Caity? A vengeance thing? Whatever it was, she felt compelled to wear the dress beside the creek early that morning, and she was murdered while wearing it.

I had told Rosenthal everything Harris told me. He gave me a sympathetic look at the time, and talked about criminals playing mind games.

Bry did not take no for an answer when it came to his invite to the Wee Goat Race.

His method of wearing me down involved a series of pics of adorable sad-face goats, texted in quick succession. Then, a short video of one of their baby goats — I was pretty sure it was Lestat — being surprised and falling into a bucket of milk. I could hear Reese's voice in the background of the video, laughing.

Yes, okay, I sent back eventually. **Give me the hard sell, why don't you. Will there be ice cream?**

Bry sent me eight ice cream emojis, then one final picture of a wobbly legged tiny goat with the biggest eyes imaginable.

See you on Sunday, I texted.

"Hey Paisley?" I called out.

Pais emerged from the kitchen. "Yessss, apprentice?" They had taken to calling me that, and found it hilarious. So far, I had set one wobbly sleeve under Paisley's direction, and made a right meal of it.

"Want to do some driving practice on Sunday?" I asked reluctantly.

Paisley's eyes lit up. "Will it take us in the direction of a certain adorable goat-themed community event?"

"Might do."

"Wooo!"

I took that as a yes.

～

"You look like a woman who does not have enough goat milk ice cream in her life," said Trace.

The The Third Annual Big Wee Goat Race went as

smoothly as anything involving the words 'goat' and 'race' possibly could.

It was a bigger crowd than I had expected. At least eight local food stalls or trucks including Reese's cake stall (with a large shade cloth to protect all the chocolate from melting) and their own brand of Wee Goat Ice Cream.

The refreshments tent was covered in cheerful bunting and contained — I had a peek in to see for myself — two dozen or so wooden chairs with absolutely no upholstery or cushioned seats whatsoever.

The locals were here, including hordes of kids at the end of a long school holiday.

The goat race itself was an intense ten minute event involving ribbons, laughter and chaos in miniature. Turns out the only way to make goats run in a reasonably straight line is for the humans to run so the goats chase them…

After that, there was a petting area set up on the shadiest side of the lower paddock for kids (and kids at heart) to meet the tiny goats (other kids!) and be taught how to gently pat them. Bry was in charge there, all grins, keeping a watchful eye over both types of kid. Paisley instantly volunteered to help, keen to squeeze out every drop of time possible with the tiny goats.

I noted with suspicion how Paisley kept dangling their sleeves into the pen as if daring the goats to take a bite. Clearly angling for some decorative bite marks to help with the visible mending project.

The goats, too good and pure for this world, defied expectation by keeping their teeth to themselves.

Mel Carmichael worked the cake and ice cream stall with Reese — she was using a walker rather than a wheelchair to assist her today. At least twice, I overheard Reese telling his mum she should take a break.

"I'm having a good day," she said impatiently. "Let me enjoy it while I can."

He looked distressed; she flicked a blob of ice cream at him.

I hadn't said hi to either of them yet. I still felt weird about it all, like I had let Reese down by staying away from the farm. Even if the crime had been resolved without my help.

(And that was without any additional awkwardness re: the steamy kiss we had shared inside a dry cleaning van.)

Clearly, the police were satisfied with Harris' arrest; the rest of the farm had no police tape across the driveway as Inspector Murphy had originally planned. It was all over bar the court case, which hopefully would in no way involve me.

I saw no police presence at all; if it was there, it was covert. There were no obvious police cars in the other paddock, the one crammed with vehicles.

I'd spotted a few familiar faces around. Guy and Annie Archer seemed to be enjoying the refreshments, though I never saw them together, only separately. Perhaps that was why they were enjoying themselves.

I even saw St John Sotheby, of all people. He had already befriended the local mayor, and ended up giving a speech and cutting a ribbon, possibly on the grounds that this was the sort of thing he expected to when he attended any kind of public fair. He had adapted somewhat to the Australian summer climate, dressed in striped shirt sleeves, light chinos and a Panama hat. I could see bright white stripes of sunscreen across his cheeks and nose, which was probably for the best.

Diana and Morgaine were here, mother and daughter driving down in Diana's convertible sports car. They held court from two of the chairs in the refreshments tent, wearing giant hats: Diana's lime green concoction looked like something out of an Audrey Hepburn film, and Morgaine's was handmade in a vintage print depicting goats playing in charming fields. I think it started out as a pair of pillow cases.

I was leaning against a fence post under the wide brim of my own excessively necessary sun hat when Trace approached with her teasing offer of goat milk ice cream. She held two giant cones of what looked a lot like raspberry ripple (my favourite flavour) and caramel fudge (her fave).

I reached for the caramel to annoy her and she darted it out of range, giving it a giant lick. "Get off. Mine."

"You are such a younger sister." I took the raspberry cone off her before she became even more of an embarrassment. "No Isaac today?"

"Work."

"On a Sunday?"

"I knew what I was getting into. It's not like we're serious yet."

"Sure."

I was 100% sure that Isaac Rosenthal was serious about literally everything, and was waiting for Trace to catch up. Still, the tough work hours would not make things easy for the two of them.

I observed Daisy idly. She was a short distance from us, explaining to several younger children how the poster on the fence for 'pin the tail on the baby goat' was not anatomically correct. I love that kid.

"What are you thinking about now?" Trace complained. "Please tell me your mind is on that flannel-clad hottie serving custard tarts and not how to source rare Bolivian buttons."

"I'm thinking about Guy and Annie' Archer's dry cleaning van," I replied.

"*Why*? It's all over, Sam. And don't think I won't hold it against you that I barely got to crack out my whiteboard this time."

Ah yes, the good old 'make a list of motive, means, opportunity' technique. The lack of distinct motives had held back my investigation for so long that the police went ahead and did their job without me.

"The thing is," I explained. "Our list of suspects was limited because there was was no way for any other person to sneak on to the property without Bandit and Chilli barking up a storm."

Isaac had not been able to find any connection between Caity O'Leary, and our small pool of suspects. If Pammy was murdered out of vengeance for her own role in Caity's death, then it was not a motive that fit Guy, Annie or Harris — and certainly not Bry or Reese.

Isaac had consulted with Sydney police again could find no death report to confirm Mel's story. Hence her being free to attend a lovely community fair, I suppose, rather than being under arrest as an accessory to a cold case of manslaughter.

Isaac was convinced Mel had made up the story about the mysterious Caity, to hide some other dodgy reason she'd disappeared when she did. I suppose I like to assume people are telling the truth, when they tell a good story.

One of many reasons I'd make a rubbish police officer.

"Oh," said Trace. "Speaking of cute dogs. Can we head home soon? I'm a bit worried that Demi's toilet training is more aspirational than successful."

"Annie!" I said out loud.

Annie Archer turned, startled to be called, and smiled when she saw me. She looked nice in another bright floral dress, though there was a crease of worry between her eyes. "Hi, Sam. You haven't been around for a while. We're off today."

"So I heard. Bit more of an exciting holiday than you planned."

"Yes, well," she sighed. "I'm not sure if we'll ever get another one. Guy keeps insisting our fortunes are about to turn around. I can't think what's got into him."

"This is my sister Trace," I said politely. "She's an estate agent."

Annie shook hands, still looking distracted. "I don't suppose you work in Launceston?"

"That's a little outside my usual patch," said Trace. "Are you looking to sell?"

"We'll have to consider it, unless — have you seen Guy anywhere?" Annie blurted out. "We were supposed to be getting on the road after that silly race. But he kept making excuses. I just walked all the way up to the cottages and back, but I didn't see him."

"We'll keep an eye out," I promised her. "We have to walk up that way ourselves."

"We do?" Trace asked as Annie wandered off in the direction of the cake stall. "I'm wearing sandals, Sam."

"I can take Paisley instead."

"Don't you dare. Dais," she called out to her daughter. "Go wait with Pais until we get back, okay?"

Daisy gave her mum a thumb's up and headed goatwards.

"Right," said Trace. "There's still some investigating to be done, then?"

"Just a little," I said.

It could be nothing. It probably was nothing. But there was something niggling at the back of my head.

I've been working on trusting my instincts lately. You don't get better at things if you don't practice.

As I led Trace out of the paddock, I heard someone say my name, and turned around. Reese was standing there, looking grumpy as usual. And handsome, obviously. Grumpily attractive. Damn it. "You came," he said, managing somehow to not give any clue in his tone whether this was a good thing or a bad thing. "Are you leaving already?"

"Just showing Trace around," I said, and introduced him quickly to my sister. "Is it okay to show her the cottages? There's no police tape or anything?"

Reese shrugged. "Nah, in the end they couldn't be bothered. Inspector Murphy reckons the case is all wrapped up. Weirdly, I think she even came to the race. I swear I spotted her earlier. Dressed casual. *Denim*."

"I can't imagine it," I said, trying not to look at his mouth.

Trace snickered next to me. I really didn't need an audience for this!

"Look, come by the stall to say hi before you head out," said Reese, ducking his head a little. "I wanted a word. If that's okay?"

"Sure, of course," I blurted.

He gave me a rare flash of a smile then headed back in the direction of his mum, and the cake stall.

Maybe not especially grumpy after all. Huh.

Trace and I watched him walk away.

"That's the brooding one?" she said.

"Yup."

"I appreciate that you waited until someone else was charged with murder before getting your flirt on. Good instincts, that Sam."

"There may have been some overlap," I winced.

"Whaaaaat! Tell me everything!"

"Come on. You can walk and shriek at the same time. Multi-tasking."

"So you don't think Harris killed Lady Whatsit?" Trace asked as we approached the cottages: The Man Cave and The Belfry standing empty. Someone had left the key in the door of the Love Shack — probably Annie and Guy when they packed up to leave.

Bandit and Chilli, chained up in the shade with plenty of water so they wouldn't disrupt the race down below, barked at us as we approached. I waved. Good dogs.

Harris' hire car had been removed, so the big white dry-cleaning van was the only vehicle there apart from the Carmichaels' ute.

"I don't know what evidence the police have managed to build against him," I admitted. "Clearly, they think he's the most likely suspect out of the small pool they have."

"Good news for Hot Farmer 1 and 2."

"And their mum, yes. Excellent news. For Annie and Guy, too."

"Come on, Sam. You don't think that tiny lady in the pretty dress strangled a person."

"It's unlikely," I admitted. "But the motive for Harris is dodgy as. — In a world of super rich people when an inconvenient relative pops up, do you really send a private investigator to kill her in a very dramatic way that actually creates a family scandal? Or is it more likely you'd send him to deliver a message — to scare her, or pay her off, to make her go away *quietly*."

Surely the police could find financial evidence that Harris had made that payment to Lady Prudence — Harris himself would be able to prove it, at least, if it came to court.

"You have a point," Trace admitted. "And here we are, scene of the crime," she sang as we approach the van. "Kissing crime. *Crime of passion*."

"Shut up, this isn't about kissing!"

She laughed at me, leaning against the van. "Go on,

then. Tell me something more interesting about this van than you making out with a cute farmer inside it."

"Okay," I said, and here was where I really was walking out on a ledge, on my own. I spoke quietly — there was no one around up here, but voices carry in the country. "This might sounds nuts, but… Guy and Annie left the property the day before Pam was killed, drove up to Hobart. They parked in town. He went off to MONA, she stayed and had coffee and did shopping. The van was unattended for hours. They never lock it, according to Guy."

Trace's eyes widened as she took in the full extent of my wild, erratic, crazy idea.

"Hang on," she said. "You don't *actually* think someone snuck into their van and hid in there for what, half a day? All night."

Yeah, it did sound stupid. "I mean, if you want to murder someone. You'd go the extra mile. Right? The murderer might not have even known about the dogs, but they surely knew that any strange vehicle in the country gets noticed. You can't sneak onto a farm by car without being seen or heard. Maybe Guy wasn't wrong about him and Annie being followed that day. This is a way someone could have got on to the property to kill Pam without being seen." I pointed at the white dry cleaning van. "Trojan horse."

Trace put her hands on her hips. "And what evidence do you think is in that van that the police who searched this place a bazillionty times didn't find?"

This was where I was potentially wasting her time and my own. "*I don't know*. Honestly, I just want to check if

I'm remembering right, if there's a space someone could have hidden in the back without being seen by the driver. Because if I'm right, the murderer could be anyone."

Anyone except our five original suspects.

But no, not anyone.

There was one person who had a really *huge* motive. And I had a horrible feeling I knew exactly who it was.

Trace narrowed her eyes at me. "And you need to check the van now because you weren't paying attention last time."

"It's possible," I admitted. "My focus was on the sewing machine."

"And the hot farm boy."

"Trace, I am regretting bringing you along!"

"Fine," she said dramatically. "Show me the scene of the crime!" And she reached out, sliding the van door open.

The face of a dead man stared back at us.

20

THE NOISE OF THE VAN DOOR SLIDING OPEN SET THE DOGS off barking again, over at the main house. I clapped a hand over Trace's mouth to stop her screaming. She made a frustrated burbling noise instead.

"Quiet," I said urgently.

This was recent. The van interior was warm, and it didn't smell great, but this had to be a recent killing, because apart from anything else, Guy Archer had been seen alive at the Third Annual Wee Goat Race, earlier today, and now he was not in any way alive.

His face was mottled and dark. His eyes bulged out of their sockets. His neck was...

Something stronger than a silk scarf, I would have thought, was used this time around. But I didn't want to think about it.

No, wait, I could see exactly what had been used. It was mostly trapped under his body. A length of red fabric, twisted into a makeshift rope.

If Guy was killed recently, that meant the killer might

still be nearby. If we were lucky, they had headed straight back to the lower paddock to shore up an alibi, putting distance between themselves and their crime.

If we weren't lucky, they were still really, really close.

"What do we do?" Trace hissed in a panic.

I took my hand away from her mouth.

"Call Isaac. Now."

No police presence at the event, as far as we knew, apart from a brief possible sighting of Inspector Murphy in casual clothes. No Isaac. If he was was working at Kingston today, or all the way over at at the Hobart station, he was too far away to be helpful.

Still, one of the lessons I've learned in more recent months is that when calling the police, you start with the ones you know.

"That's a dead body, Sam," Trace said shakily, making a call on her phone.

"It's Guy," I told her.

"Oh, poor Annie," she said immediately. "Wait. Did the wife do it?"

It would take a particularly strong person to strangle a bloke that solid. Or someone very, very scary.

Not Annie, surely. I could not imagine it.

"We're going to head back to the crowd," I told Trace. I felt weirdly calm. "We'll be safe there, until the police come."

"He's not picking up," she said impatiently, waving her phone at me.

"Text him while we walk."

"What do I say?"

"Tell him there's been another murder. Type the name Caity, with a C."

"The old roommate? The one Pam killed with a typewriter?"

This was it, my big theory. Time to look stupid.

"Caitlyn O'Leary. I don't think she's dead," I admitted. "Isaac couldn't find any evidence of a body found in Sydney at the right time. He assumed Mel made the story up about Caity. If Mel was telling the truth, but she only *thought* Caity died, then Caity herself is the one person with an actual solid motive to murder Pammy."

She could be nearby. She could look like *anyone*. I didn't want to scare Trace more than I already had, but we needed to get out of here.

"What makes you think she's alive?" Trace asked as we headed away from the van at a sharp walking pace.

I'd wondered before. But now… now, I was afraid that it had to be true.

"The person who killed Guy twisted a whole dress up to use as a weapon. A familiar, red dress. The one Paisley and I made is in police evidence. The original dress — according to Mel, Caity was wearing it when Pam hit her with a typewriter and they escaped. Fifteen years ago."

Trace shoved her phone in her pocket, looking resolute. "So we run?"

"Stick with walking quickly."

I was tempted to run over and release the dogs. Safety in numbers. But, no. No diversions or delays. Our job right now was to very calmly walk down this dirt road until we were surrounded by people.

"It doesn't fit," Trace said, as we neared the farm-house, walking quickly over the gravel.

"What do you mean?"

"This Caity person might have snuck on to the property in the van like you said, if she was extra enough to stalk Guy and Annie, then hide in a van for twelve hours or whatever. But how did she get off the property *after* killing Pam? The police searched everywhere, that day. And like, lots of times later. What was she, up a tree the whole time?"

"Walk faster," I urged.

I'd thought about that too. Bry told me on the first day that there were electric fences between here and the other properties. Every gate had security cameras. The police had checked all that footage. It was unlikely, but not impossible, that a determined person had managed to doctor the cameras, or replace the footage, or something.

Right now, though, as my mind flooded with adrenalin, with certainty that Caity was the one who killed both Pam and Guy, I remembered something: Bry had specifically told me that Inspector Murphy checked the footage herself. Inspector Murphy, who was tall and scary and around the same age as both of our Prue Scythes.

Inspector Murphy, who stepped out of the farmhouse as we passed it, holding something in a plastic carry bag.

Reese was right: she was wearing casual clothes today. Jeans and a peach coloured t-shirt that looked like it had been ironed, with a white linen shirt hanging open like a jacket. She shared at us both, startled.

"Oh thank goodness," said Trace. "Look, Sam, the police are here already. It's Lyn, isn't it?" she said to

Inspector Murphy. "We met at that fundraising ball last month. I'm Isaac Rosenthal's girlfriend."

Lyn. Caitlyn. Caity. Did no one keep the same name they'd used in their 20s?

"We're just heading back down," I said, hoping Trace's innocence would work for us here. "Have you tried the goat milk ice cream yet?"

Inspector Murphy's face was grim. "I heard the dogs bark."

"We disturbed them," said Trace immediately, and I knew that she had realised what was happening. "My fault. Got stung by an ant. Those horrible bull ants. I'm allergic. Better get to the first aid tent…"

Murphy moved quickly, drawing a service weapon from under her white linen shirt. "I think you'd better get into the van," she said, with a frightening calm. "Don't you, Samantha? But first, I want you to give me your phones."

Don't let them take you to a second location.

Isaac's idea of a birthday present was self defence classes, for me and for Trace. We'd rolled our eyes at the time, but it was actually kind of fun, and I took it as tacit endorsement of my new (semi) career as a detective.

The third class was titled How To Avoid Abduction.

In the first five minutes after Inspector Murphy turned her service weapon on me and Trace, I think we broke like, all the rules we learned in that class.

Except for the Don't Die one that the instructor

solemnly told us at the end. "Do what you have to, stall for as long as you can, wait for help. The longer you stay alive, the more hope there is that someone will get to you in time."

So, we stayed alive. We did what she said.

But no one got to us in time.

Murphy made me drive. She took the passenger seat. All the better to hold her gun low in her lap. She had both our phones shoved in a pocket of her linen shirt, where neither of us could reach them.

The paddock was still full of people and festivities as I brought the van slowly down the gravel drive. I paused for as long as I could, at the end of the driveway before turning on to the road, hoping to catch someone's eye. Hoping that Reese or Bry or Annie or St John Bloody Sotheby (probably not him) would notice the van, and recognise that it shouldn't be here. Shouldn't be leaving the property.

"Get moving," Murphy hissed. She shifted in her seat, pointing her gun away from me, back into the van.

Trace was back there, not even strapped in, precariously perched alongside the dead body of Guy. I couldn't risk doing anything stupid, crashing the van to escape.

No, we were well and truly going to a second location. Go us.

I checked my mirrors, turned, and drove away from Wee Goat Farm.

If anyone noticed us, I didn't see them noticing.

My entire focus was on keeping me and Trace alive for the next five minutes. Then five minutes after that. Whatever it took. That probably meant not annoying our abductor.

"Why did you kill him?" Trace asked a minute later. Clearly, she had not been paying attention during the How To Avoid Abduction class.

"Be quiet," snarled Murphy as we pulled on to the Huon Highway, heading north, towards the saddle, and Kingston and, after that, the city of Hobart. "I didn't bring you for conversation."

"Seriously, though," I said a few minutes later. "Don't tell me he figured out who killed Pam on his own." I might have to quit detecting altogether if Guy Archer of all people was better at it than me.

"He found the scarf," the killer said sullenly. "I hid it under his sewing machine during the first police search. He must have found it straight away, realised I was the only one who could have done it. Believe me, I wasn't expecting him to be that smart either."

It was hard not to sympathise with someone who found Guy annoying, until I reminded myself that she had murdered him.

"So Guy put it in the attic?"

"He thought he could blackmail me for money," she said abruptly. "Me! I'm next in line to be Chief Inspector."

Not anymore, probably. Unless she got rid of me and Trace without having further suspicion fall on her.

I needed to stop thinking about that possibility, or there was no way I could drive the van safely.

"Okay." I was going to have to put this together. It

gave me something to focus on, while keeping my hands steady on the wheel. "So that night, the night you killed her. Did you really follow Guy's van, sneak inside and stay hidden inside all night? That's a thing you did?"

"It was unexpected," Murphy said haughtily. "I had another plan to park nearby and hike to the property. But when they left their van unattended, I took the opportunity."

It didn't sound like something you did accidentally. "How did you even know Pam was connected to Guy and Annie?"

"I've always kept an eye on Mel and her boys," said Inspector Murphy with a sly sort of smile that chilled me to the bone. "She was the greatest danger to me after I was transferred to the Hobart office. It's such a small city. There's always the possibility of running into an old friend. So I made sure to avoid it."

"How?"

"I'm good at my job," she said, which almost sounded like a non-sequitur. "It's tough to get advancement, as a woman in the police service. Let alone a woman over fifty. Unlike many of my colleagues, I keep up with all the advancements in modern technology. Mel Carmichael doesn't exchange an email or a text message without me knowing about it."

Yep. Definitely creepy. "So, you knew when Pam got in touch with her?"

"Oh, Pammy. Imagine my surprise. She'd kept her distance all these years and suddenly she was talking about not only visiting Mel in Tasmania, but pitching a documentary about the True Prue Scythe story. I couldn't have that. I'd lucked out when they didn't go to the police, the first time around. But the career I built for myself, after that bitch tried to kill me with a typewriter? I wasn't willing to lose it just so Pammy could tell her story."

"You knew Pam was staying at the farm. You staked it out?"

"Police skills in action," said Inspector Murphy, with a disturbing smile. "I rather miss the early days. Stakeouts and takedowns. It's mostly office work, for me now. With the occasional juicy murder, of course, to liven things up."

"Was the plan always to kill Pam?"

"The plan was to stop her," said Murphy, terribly calm. "I couldn't let her tell the story of what happened at that beach house fifteen years ago. She might be the one who assaulted me, but I wouldn't come out of the story well."

No, I couldn't imagine she would, what with the kidnap and everything.

"Were you going to kill Mel as well? The boys' mother?"

"I hadn't decided yet. If it needed to be done."

We were up past the saddle of the mountain now, heading around the turns. I was travelling as slowly as I dared, well aware that Trace had no seat belt. As the road straightened out ahead of me, I saw some kind of obstruction up ahead. I wasn't sure what it was, but I didn't like the look of it. "Trace, are you okay?" I asked, hoping to distract Murphy.

"I'm fine," said Trace, popping up behind my car seat. A little too close to the inspector's gun for my liking. "That was smart of you," she told Murphy, taking the lead on distracting her. Smart cookie, my sister. "Getting on to the property without being seen. And you got away later, I suppose, because you were the one who seized the security footage."

"That part was easy," said Murphy, eyes Trace and not me.

"How did you make sure she wore dress?" Trace asked, with faked enthusiasm.

"Oh, I know that part," I said, remembering my conversation with Harris from the Remand Centre. "You sent her the dress. And a phone. I assume you were threatening her, sending stalkery messages."

"I'd love to see you prove that," said Inspector Murphy, in a voice that made it clear she was delighted that I had figured out that particular detail. She was *proud* of this whole production. "I had to make sure she was too scared to say anything about me."

"Creepy messages on a secret phone. That was enough, you know," I told her. "She accepted the payout from her family to stop making the film, the night before you pulled that business with the van. Probably because you'd already freaked her out. You could have stopped there."

Murphy scoffed. "As if she was going to stop making her film. *The Prue Scythe Story*. What a joke. She wasn't even the real Prue Scythe. I sent her instructions. She was to accept a video call wearing the dress I sent her, at a specific time. I didn't think she'd be so dramatic as to go outside to do it," she added with a groan. "I was expecting to collect her from the cottage. That idiot Archer had left his keys in the van. I was going to make Pammy get into the van, drive her somewhere else, ditch the van and her in a lake. I had a *plan*."

"But Pammy went for an early morning stroll," I said thoughtfully.

"Ridiculous woman. She always had to be dramatic," said the woman with the gun.

Police cars up ahead, I was sure of it. Cars were slowed and stopping. I eased on my own brakes.

"She was following your instructions, though. You had her so scared, she cut up the dress to make last minute alterations, so she'd definitely be wearing it when you called."

If only she'd taken someone into her confidence. Harris would have gone with her, or advised her to take the call in a public place.

(Guy, of course, she must have told him something in order to borrow his sewing machine. But he had been the wrong person, clearly was never going to be unselfish enough to support her.)

"Why are you slowing down?" Murphy snapped, eyes back on the road. "Keep going."

"I can't," I said desperately. "Look, they're stopping all cars. I can't get through. Breathalyser station maybe?"

Police everywhere, up ahead of us. She couldn't miss that.

Murphy raised her gun, pointing it at me, at least, and not my sister. "Keep driving."

There was nowhere to go, cars backed up along the highway. Too many of them, between us and the police cars. I put more pressure on the brakes, wanting to close my eyes. "Sorry," I said, which was ridiculous.

She was the one about to shoot me. Why was I the one apologising?

As the car pulled to stop in the middle of the highway, Inspector Murphy let out a wheezing, gasping sound that I realised too late was a laugh.

I saw police walking up the dry and dusty side of the highway towards us — uniformed officers. For once, I wasn't terrified to see them. And oh, Rosenthal. Inspector Isaac Rosenthal was with them.

"At least no one hit me with a typewriter this time," said Murphy dryly. There was that sense of humour again, coming out in rare moments, like a surprise brick through the window.

As I sat frozen behind the wheel of the van, she very carefully laid her gun on the dashboard, and put both of her hands behind her head.

21

"WE WERE LUCKY," ROSENTHAL SAID GRIMLY, MUCH
later in the day, as we gathered on Great Aunt Harriet's
back verandah. He couldn't stop touching Trace — a hand
on her arm, her shoulder. It was the most PDA I'd seen
from him for the length of their entire relationship.

I knew the feeling. I wanted to wrap her in a doona and
hug her for the next five years or so.

Daisy, amazingly untraumatised, was happily playing
with Paisley and the puppy.

I couldn't stop thinking about how close we had come
to Daisy having a very different kind of day.

The Fashionably Late family squashed together on the
veranda, with a couple of kitchen chairs to make room for
Morgaine and Diana, and their extraordinarily large hats.

"Very impressed you pulled a police barricade together
so quickly," said Morgaine.

"The highway breathalyser patrol were already set up
near Sandfly," said Rosenthal. "I was on the road from
Kingston when I missed Trace's call. Like I said, *lucky*. I

was able to get to the highway patrol in time to slow traffic and keep an eye out for that white van."

"But who alerted you to what was happening?" I asked. "Who saw us leaving with Inspector Murphy?"

"Me!" called out Paisley, dodging Daisy and Demi long enough to come and collapse on the deck, red-faced. "Pimms me, Sam."

I passed Paisley a glass of bright red Pimms and lemonade, poured from a large glass jug with strawberries and oranges floating in it. "You saw the van?"

"I saw you driving it," they said. "Annie spotted it first. Reese saw Inspector Murphy in the passenger seat. He made me call *our* Inspector."

"Good work," I said. I hadn't spoken Reese since our exchange in the paddock. No calls or texts. I suppose he had things to do. Family dramas to sort out. Cakes to put away in the fridge.

I hadn't messaged him, either.

"And me!" said Trace. "I texted Isaac sneakily. I told him she had a gun and two hostages."

"You did," he said, kissing her on the top of the head. "Some of the words even came through comprehensibly."

"I was typing one-handed with the phone inside my handbag."

"You have many skills," he said generously.

"Wait," I said. "Murphy took your phone."

Trace rolled her eyes. "Who only has one phone, Sam? I'm kidding," she added, laughing at me. "I had Daisy's in my bag, because she got ice cream on it."

"I suppose this means Mark Harris is innocent," I said suddenly. "Are you going to let him go?"

"Since we arrested him for the murder of Lady Prudence and it turned out his arresting officer was actually responsible for that death," said Inspector Rosenthal, wincing. "I'm sure due process and his very expensive team of lawyers will sort it all out."

"He was helpful, you know," I reminded him.

Rosenthal conceded the point with a nod. "I'm sure Harris will be firmly encouraged to return to his country of origin as swiftly as possible, and that the charges against him will be lifted. Personally, I'd love to get several members of the Sotheby family on conspiracy charges for sending him here in the first place, but I don't think Australian justice is going to have a look in there."

The doorbell rang.

Trace, cozy in the arms of her inspector, put her finger on her nose. "You get it, Sam."

"Fine," I grumbled, getting to my feet.

Aunt Harriet's cottage was blissfully cool as I walked through it, away from the sunny back yard.

I couldn't say who I was hoping to find, standing on our doorstep, but it wasn't the younger son of an Earl. St John Sotheby was still in his shirtsleeves, though he had wiped off the sunscreen.

"Ah," he proclaimed in an accent far too posh to belong in this century. "The inestimable Samantha Sullivan."

"That's a compliment, right?" I couldn't help myself. Something about the outrageous Englishness of him made me want to dial my own accent up the full ocker. If I spent more than five minutes with him, I was going to end up talking like Crocodile Dundee.

"I believe I owe you a little something for clearing up the matter of my sister's murder." He handed me an envelope made from paper so soft that it might have been created from like, silkworms and merino wool. Or very, very fancy trees, I suppose.

"News travels fast," I said, feeling super awkward about this. "It wasn't exactly a tidy piece of detective work on my part. I got held hostage by accident, and the police cleared up most of the, uh, matter."

He raised his eyebrows at me. They were perfectly shaped, as if recently plucked. "I understand the police arrested the wrong person and then, after your involvement, arrested the correct person. I'm perfectly content with paying your fee for a job well done."

I fumbled with the envelope. "I'm sure anyone could have… HOLY CHRISTMAS."

That was. That was a big cheque. That was a *Sam gets a new car* cheque. "Thank you for hiring the Fashion Detectives," I said with a bright smile, very quickly. "How do you feel about a glass of Pimms and lemonade?"

"Charmed and enthusiastic," St John Sotheby drawled.

Out of the corner of my eye, I saw a ute with two very familiar dogs drive past the house, parking further up the road where there were plenty of spots in front of the playground.

"Okay," I said, opening the door wider. "Head on through to the back deck, Isaac Rosenthal can introduce you to everyone. I'll be along in a minute."

St John Sotheby gave me a head bob and a smirk that suggested he was thinking about kissing my hand, or something equally swoonworthy. Then he ducked his head and went inside Aunt Harriet's cottage.

I shoved the *internal shrieking sound* cheque into one of the deep pockets of my sun dress, and ran across the road to where Reese Carmichael was leaning against his ute, with Chilli and Bandit lolling around in the back tray. He'd found a shady spot, and they did not look like they wanted to move at all. They didn't even bark at me.

"I'd invite you in," I said breathlessly. "But Daisy has a puppy and I don't think he's ready to be around full sized dogs yet."

"That's okay," said Reese. "I can't stay long. Left Mum and Bry consoling Annie around the kitchen table. At some point, they're going to need someone to feed them all."

"Ducks," I said as the local troops began to circle, quacking half-heartedly at us. "Um. There's a dog beach around the corner?"

"I know it well," said Reese. For once his face didn't have a trace of its default state of grumpiness. His eyes were warm, and I could feel the anticipation of something between us. "Lead the way."

We walked, following the river around the long bend to the dog beach beyond, with Chilli and Bandit happily roaming on their leashes ahead of us. They ducked in and out of the shallow waters, getting thoroughly mucky with grit and salt. That was definitely a Reese problem for the future, not a Sam problem, so I enjoyed watching them play.

"Poor Annie," I thought to say. "How's she doing?"

"She's been crying," said Reese, with a slightly hunted expression. "But then she stops crying and looks cheerful, and then she feels guilty and then she starts crying again. All way beyond my pay grade."

"So you left her to your mother."

"To Bry," he said defensively. "Who has like, 80% of our family's collective emotional intelligence."

"It's good to be self-aware about these things."

"Annie has a niece who's coming down to look after her. And take her home, hopefully, tomorrow, since her vehicle has been impounded."

I shuddered a bit, thinking about Guy's large, ungainly body flopping around the back of his van. I think, if I'd been married to someone like that, I'd also be feeling secretly cheerful about my future now he had been murdered. Like Annie, I would definitely feel bad about feeling secretly cheerful.

"Meanwhile," said Reese, who also had an air of secret cheerfulness about him. "All our guests for the next two weeks have cancelled their bookings. No one's looking for the authentic murder farm experience right now."

"That sounds like a bad thing," I said sternly.

"Sounds like a holiday," he said fervently, then held my gaze for a moment. "We had a bit of a talk, me and Mum and Bry, while there was all the — everything, going on. We put it all out there. What we each want from the family business."

"And?"

"And. Well. Turns out that Mum has been going out of her head stuck in town, and she wants to come back to live on the property, at least for the next couple of years, depending on how her health holds up. We also want her close until the court case — all the Prue Scythe stuff is going to come out one way or another."

I didn't ask again, if he had known all along who she was. Honestly, I didn't think so. One way or another, he had clearly had to process a lot of new revelations about his mother's past over the last week.

"She's agreed to leave the physical jobs to Bry," Reese went on. "We're looking to get some carer support in when she needs it. Dropping the place in town will free up some income to get the rest of the accessibility renovations done, too."

"You're okay with her coming home?"

"Yeah," he said, looking like a weight had been lifted off his shoulders. "Glad she told us. No wonder things have been weird with her pretending everything was fine for the last year. Speaking of — Bry hasn't been happy either."

I knew all that wild bounciness had to be hiding something. "Oh, really?"

"He knows he's more invested in the farm business than I am. But because I'm the oldest, he always feels like he has to run everything past me. And I'm not exactly…"

"Mr Positivity?" I suggested tactfully.

"Exactly. We've agreed Bry will be sole farm manager. No weddings or big catering events, apart from the annual goat race, obviously."

"Obviously!"

"He'll focus on the B&B and expanding the dairy, I'll chip in with the ice cream production but otherwise I'll keep my oar out of farm decisions. The business ones, anyway. Still planning to complain loudly about decisions that affect those of us living on site. I'll be able to take on some projects away away from the farm, give Bry some space. A friend of mine is doing a pop-up restaurant in Cygnet next month. Wants me to come on board as pastry chef."

"And that's doable, is it?"

"If we put a hold on the plans to expand our accommodation and event space and focus on the businesses we currently have — the cottages, and the goats, then yeah. My income will be more useful than my labour."

"It's been a big day," I noted.

He smiled at me. It was probably a good thing he spent most of the time being grumpy, because the effect of a happy, Reese Carmichael was devastating. Like a tidal wave, but in a good way. "It's a start. Probably going to end in disaster, but at least we're talking about it now. How are things with you?"

"Calming down. Recovering." With a giant cheque burning a hole in my pocket. "Improving rapidly, as it happens."

We walked in silence for a while, across the damp sand, as other people with their various dogs circled and spiralled around us. It was heading into evening, and the tide was coming in. All the more waves for dogs to play with.

"You'll be pretty busy," I noted. "Pop-up restaurants, ice cream, renovations, all those tiny goats around to distract you with their cuteness."

"I will," Reese conceded. "I'll, uh, have some evenings

free, though. I expect. Now I don't have to upholster chairs or rage-bake any wedding cakes."

"Oh," I said with a small smile. "And what will do you do with all that free time?"

He gave a sweep of his hand, indicating the beach and the dogs and well, me. "More of this, I hope."

I stopped, my feet sinking into the sand. "You're going to have to be more specific."

He stopped too, turning to face me, crowding in close in a way that only makes sense if you're about to kiss someone. "Want a list?"

"I have a whiteboard and some markers somewhere if that would be helpful—"

His hands were sandy and damp from the dog's leashes. I didn't mind at all, when he cupped my face and drew me in.

It was a good start.

Some time later, with the sky finally starting to darken after a spectacular sunset, I returned alone to the very festive back verandah of Aunt Harriet's little house. My family and co-workers and the puppy and the son of an earl were all quite merry by now, with a new platter of nibbles to pick at. The Pimms jug was empty, but there was still orange juice, and a half-empty bottle of sparkling white.

Apparently, the Sam and Trace Escaped An Abduction gathering was now a party.

When there was a lull between conversation, refreshments and puppy antics, I drew Paisley aside and showed them the check from St John Sotheby.

"Whoa!" they exclaimed.

"I know. Obviously we'll split it."

Paisley gave me a skeptical look. "He didn't hire *me*."

"He hired the Fashion Detectives, that's both of us."

"Yeah," Paisley said, sounding awkward. "I've been thinking about that. What happened to you and Trace today, that was — real. Really real."

"Too real?" I suggested gently.

Paisley hesitated, then nodded. "I'm not sure the whole Fashion Detective thing is a me thing after all. I know I started it! But I think maybe — fashion, not detective. Focus on what I'm good at. One thing at a time."

"That's okay," I said, shoving the cheque back in my pocket. I'd figure out how to make sure they got their share when things were less fraught. "I've been thinking, too. I should be all in or all out, you know? Properly apply for an private investigator license, or let it drop and go back to setting sleeves."

"You do need a lot of practice in setting sleeves," Paisley said gravely. "So which is it, fashion or detective?"

I really loved working at Fashionably Late. But I liked nosing around and fixing people's problems, too. Technically, working at the boutique was still only a part-time job. That left a lot of free time, only a small amount of which was likely to be dedicated to walking on beaches with a grumpy pastry chef and his dogs.

"I didn't say I was going to choose between them," I said finally. "I can do more than one thing if I want to. As long as I do them properly. So, yes. I'm applying for my private investigation license, and I am keeping the Fashion Detective name, because it pays to specialise. *And* I want to improve on my dressmaking skills, so you're not losing an apprentice."

"Awesome," said Paisley. "Next time you have a murder to solve, I will be right there in the support team, holding a whiteboard, making cups of tea and not getting abducted by killers."

"Oh, there will be no more murder," I insisted. "Detective yes, murder no. I'll be taking on small scale investigations only."

After all, how often was a fashion-related murders likely to fall into my lap?

END

ABOUT THE AUTHOR

Livia Day lives in Tasmania, an island state of Australia where she plots all her murders.

If you like your dead bodies with a side of cake, you may enjoy the delicious Cafe La Femme series:

- *A Trifle Dead*
- *Drowned Vanilla*
- *The Blackmail Blend (free short story)*
- *Keep Calm and Kill the Chef*

Join Livia's monthly newsletter:
https://mailchi.mp/tansyrr/liviaday

I would like to thank Z.E. Davidson & Carolyn for their helpful goat notes & feedback to help make the farm scenes (and baking!) a little more authentic.

This book was written on lutrawita (Tasmania) Aboriginal land. I acknowledge, with deep respect, the traditional owners of this land, the palawa people.